# D.O.D.

# D.O.D.

BY LYNNE ALLSBROW

**DORRANCE PUBLISHING CO., INC.**
PITTSBURGH, PENNSYLVANIA 15222

This is a work of fiction. Names, characters, places, and incidents are either the product of the author's imagination or are used fictitiously, and any resemblance to actual persons, living or dead; events; or locales is entirely coincidental.

Author's note: Some people, places, and events in this book are real and some are not. Thank you to the people who gave me permission and who provided me details about their lives, places, names, and events. The author has taken writer's privilege to create a story and to change some details.

ISBN: 978-0-8059-7657-1

Printed in the United States of America

*First Printing*

For more information or to order additional books, please contact:
Dorrance Publishing Co., Inc.
701 Smithfield Street
Third Floor
Pittsburgh, Pennsylvania 15222
U.S.A.
1-800-788-7654
*www.dorrancebookstore.com*

Dedicated to:

MTK

# CHAPTER 1

He lay on the floor at the end of the day in the dark, cigarette smoke rising up—a glass of water on the table beside him. The only light came from the television where an erotic movie was showing that all forms of having sex were "natural." He believed that. This was his favorite time of day—alone time. Here, in his room, there were no decisions to make, no yelling at the crew, no equipment to move, no deadlines to meet. The bridge builder was very good at what he did, and he made no bones about letting people know he thought so.

Just last Thursday he heard Mike say, "Dax Mason is a hard worker and he will run your ass ragged, but he won't make you do anything he wouldn't do. All you have to do is keep up." The new hire, Kevin, father of two, not married to their mother, just looked at Dax and took another sip of beer.

"You got your own tools?" Dax asked.

"What kind of tools?" Kevin asked.

"A level, straight edge, cordless drill, hammer," Dax shot back.

"You know, I have my neck stickin' out real far by hiring you with no experience, but you told me your story and that's why I hired you. I'll loan you a hundred bucks to get some tools and you can pay me back." Dax—the giver, the taker.

Dax learned the bridge building business when he was a young boy back in Indiana. At seventeen, he worked part-time on weekends. The next year, he added working after school too. His apprenticeship was what you would call "hands-on" and "hold on to your ass" while it's getting chewed off. The five old guys (mid-forties) who taught Dax the ropes didn't mince words. If you f—d up, you weren't forgiven. Dax learned quickly that you did the work right the first time or suffered the consequences. You redid the work

1

yourself—no help. You did it over and over again until you got it right. From this experience, Dax learned that a hard day of work was the best satisfaction he would get in his life, and no one could take that away from him. And so, he put more hours in on the jobs than anyone else just to prove to himself and others that he was going to be the best. Dax has been doing this work now for twenty-five years.

His first big job was in Chicago. He learned more aspects of what it took to actually build a bridge. He watched and remembered the critical pieces of setting the rebar, laying the Styrofoam so the bridge could breathe, making the reinforcements, and pouring the girders under the bridge. By the time Dax left the Chicago area, he had become a foreman and knew what it took to build a bridge that would last years. People's lives depended on Dax knowing his job.

When Dax was in his mid-twenties, he went to Colorado on vacation to visit his sister. He ended up staying. It was while he was working on the Glenwood Canyon project that he met Nyckie. They lived together for two years before getting married. He met her in a bar, which was where they spent a lot of their time together. The only free time he allowed himself was on the weekends. The strain of his work commitment took its toll quickly on his marriage. He and Nyckie had two children right away, Dade and Solei. He didn't really talk about why he slept on the couch or with the children the last three years they were married, but the divorce was final by the end of six years. Nyckie left Colorado and took the children back to Illinois so she could be closer to her parents.

This job took him north of Denver. The Hwy 36 and Federal overpass needed to be replaced and widened. The city of Westminster contracted to have the bridge made into four lanes with new on-and-off ramps. This was to be topped off by adding four vanity structures on top for appearance. All of which had to be pre-built in wooden forms made by hand. By 5:30 AM he was on the job site reading the paper, drinking coffee, smoking cigarettes, and making small talk with the guys arriving onto the site. The daily get-your-ass-in-gear meeting was about to begin.

"Damn, it's gonna be another 95 degree day." Roger complained about the weather a lot.

He and Dax had worked together for over thirteen years now, twelve years on the Glenwood Canyon project and one year on this one.

"Yep, don't let your hair stick to your balls, cause today we gotta keep movin'", he said, smiling at Roger. "The concrete will be here by 8:00 AM so we gotta have all the rods and reinforcements in place and the first batch ready to pour by 7:30 AM."

The day went fast and everyone had sweat-stained T-shirts. Dax's shirt had the word SPAM imprinted over a can of Spam on it. (Dax really likes Spam!) One of his bar buddies gave him this great shirt. Dax's bar friends were his family now. They accepted him for the way his was: sometimes crude, sometimes funny, and most times a hard-ass. They knew him as the guy who would give you money when you need it, work at your house for free, or fill in at the bar when need be. This was the unselfish Dax. He never asked for anything in return. So his friends took the bad with the good.

After the Glenwood Project, he moved closer to Denver to find more work and bigger projects. Denver was where Dax had his first encounter with ICO. Dax was sitting on a bench near the art museum downtown, people watching. A man with a dog approached him. The man asked Dax if he would hold his dog's leash while he got something from the car. Dax said, "Sure, what's the dog's name?"

"Shan," the man said not looking back.

Within a minute, a police car drove up, two cops jumped out of the car, pulled their weapons and yelled at Dax to get on the ground. When Dax was spread-eagle on the ground, they handcuffed him and stuffed him in the back of the police car. The dog was gone. Dax was taken to a building on the 16th Street mall in lower downtown with the name, "SUGAR" on the front. He was questioned for hours about a drug deal that was going down which he knew nothing about. When his interrogators finally realized they had the wrong target, they quickly ushered Dax out of the building and sent him off in a cab.

Normally, Dax would have let this go, but not this time. The next day, he went back to the building and demanded to talk to someone inside about what had happened to him yesterday. Several minutes passed. Finally a man who looked like a model in a GQ magazine introduced himself as Brand Carlson and told Dax to follow him. The conversation was brief. Dax was told a mistake had been made and that the man they were looking for was the owner of the dog. Something in Dax clicked. He said if they had done their research, they would have known that Dax did not own a dog. Dax offered to go back to the park and be a decoy so they could catch the real guy. This is how Dax became part of the ICO team.

The ICO (Interception Communication Office) had been in existence for twenty years when Dax first signed on as an Information Distribution Analyst. The organization didn't have high-tech surveillance in the early years. Dax's job was to decide where the hot spots in the world would appear next—drug trafficking, assassination attempts, hijackings.

The information would come to him in all forms: phone calls, faxes, US mail, flowers with cards, flyers on his windshield, napkins dropped on his dining table, ads in the newspaper, or panhandlers on the street. He never learned how the people giving him their secrets knew where he would be and when, but they always found him. At first, when strangers approached him, he tried to ask how they knew where and when to reach him, but no one would talk. So, before long, he accepted the interactions as normal.

Dax moved up quickly in the organization mostly due to his skills, but also because his boss, General Carlson, believed in him and saw to it that Dax had exposure for his successes. Carlson's position was well-known to everyone in the business. He had no use for formality. He was only addressed by his first name. Brand loved this job and took a special interest in Dax on their first assignment together in El Centro, California, in 1976. They walked across the border to Mexicali, where children were begging on the street and others were asleep on the sidewalk in clothes that should be burned. They walked up and down the street lined with souvenir shops. Occasionally Brand would go into a shop and make small talk with the store clerks. Dax walked over to a food vendor and bought a "homemade" taco.

"You really gonna eat that?" Brand asked.

"Yeah, looks great don't it?" Dax asked as the grease ran down his arm.

After about an hour, Brand said, "Well, let's head back."

"What the heck were we supposed to do here anyway?"

"Never mind" was the only answer he got back.

As they were nearing the border, Dax reached down to pull a blanket over the bare legs of a little girl sleeping on the sidewalk next to her mother.

"Freeze, Señor, or I will blow your head off." Dax froze long enough to hear the end of the sentence. In the next second, Dax had placed his leg behind the gunman's ankle and brought his attacker's body down hard on the cement, his head hitting first. At the same time, Brand grabbed the young girl and started running back towards the border.

"Wait! Don't you want to take the target?"

"I have the target," Brand yelled back as he kept running.

Dax caught up just as they reached the border. The girl was wide-awake now. She didn't struggle or say a word.

"Let me do the talking," Brand whispered to Dax. "Good afternoon, officer. As you can see my friend and I need to take my sister's child to a hospital. She is covered with open sores and suffers from exposure to the weather."

"You have identification?"

"Yes, of course." Brand handed the girl over to Dax. To Dax's amazement, Brand produced their passports along with the girl's birth certificate and power of legal guardianship.

"Proceed. Next!" the officer said as he turned his attention to the next person in line.

They walked for several blocks without speaking. Dax knew enough Spanish to tell the girl she was safe and everything would be better soon. When they were in the car headed back to San Diego, Dax finally asked, "So she was the target?"

"Yes, the man you put in a coma was after her, not you."

"Why her? She is just a homeless kid on the street. What could she possibly know?"

Brand smiled to himself. He loved training new agents. "It is not what she knows; it is what is tattooed on her body." They drove the rest of the way in silence.

By the time they reached the home office in San Diego, the girl was asleep again. They stopped only once to get something to eat. The hamburger and fries from the In and Out drive-thru were eaten quickly by the girl. They were met at the door by a team of doctors and nurses who quickly took the girl to a hospital emergency room in the basement of the office building. They gave her a light sedative to relax her. She accepted everything they did to her.

When they removed her clothing, they could hardly stand to look at her mutilated body. Not only was she covered with open, infested sores, she also had a series of small burns in the shape of crosses that encircled a tattoo on her back. A perfect replica of a twenty dollar bill had been burned into her skin. Dax and Brand watched through the glass as the team began to decipher the code using high-powered magnification that was projected onto a wide screen. Names and numbers began showing up throughout the imprint. That was the last Dax ever saw of the little girl and was the last Dax would learn about that assignment. Everything at ICO was on a need-to-know basis.

ICO was very protective of their agents. They would contact Dax every month or two when they needed him. After each job, Dax returned to his bridge building work. Every time Dax returned from an ICO job, it took him a few days to forget what he had just experienced. He threw himself into his work and made the crew wish he had been gone longer.

"So, Dax, how's it goin'?"

"What? You got time to sit around and shoot the shit with me?"

Kevin winced, "Well, no, but..."

"Then get your ass back to work."

"Geez, don't you have a decent bone in your body?"

"Bite me" was Dax's reply as Kevin slammed the trailer door on his way out.

When the day was over and Dax was sitting on the barstool, he drank a shot of Wild Turkey first and then ordered his usual, rum and Coke with a twist of lime. This was Dax's life and he liked it just that way.

# CHAPTER 2

Dax's job as a bridge builder was physically satisfying to him. He liked his routine: Up at 4:30 AM (his clock was always ten minutes fast), on the job by 5:15 AM and everyone and everything where it was supposed to be before the sun was completely up. Dax didn't go to lunch with the guys either. He went to the trailer, worked on time cards, or made calls about supplies or equipment. At the end of his day, to unwind he would go to J R's Silver Bullet and drink with his buddies. He had a $1,000 bar tab there. Everyone knew the owner as JR. He was named after his father, Isador Bueno Jr., the patron saint of the farmer. All of his father's family were named after saints. JR had gotten to know Dax over the years. Dax was good for the money. He drank and talked till about 7:00 PM, then would slip out the back without saying good-bye. That was Dax's life—groundhog day Monday through Friday—at least that is how it appeared to everyone else.

Because Dax had the most bridge building experience than anyone on his crew, he was often called away from his site to go put out a fire on other jobs in the area. Asphalt Specialties was a large company owned by the Hunt brothers, which employed people from all walks of life. There was Rudy, who only had one eye. There was John, who was Dax's right-hand man. John knew what it took to build anything in the way of materials. He made sure the inventory, supplies, fuel, and all the materials Dax needed were there when Dax needed them. And then there was Mike, the carpenter. Mike was diagnosed with stomach cancer last year. He gave himself his own morphine shots for the pain. He did not want to stop working. Most of the rest of the crew were Hispanics who didn't speak much English.

Dax could relate to them all in a way they understood. He didn't talk to them the way his foreman did when he was learning the business. Dax was

6

the old man in his middle forties now, training the younger crew. Times were different today—well, sort of. Some things in this tough way of making a living stayed the same. One hidden rule was, if you were a new guy and you didn't say the word F—k in the first five minutes, you were considered gay. The crew all liked Dax. They felt safe when Dax was around, cause they could always go to Dax when they didn't know what to do or when things broke down.

It was not unusual for Dax to be gone from his site for hours at a time. No one questioned Dax of his whereabouts. They knew what his answer would be, "None of your damn business." Only three people who knew Dax as a builder of bridges knew about Dax's life as an ICO agent—Dax's Asphalt Specialties boss, Roger, his ICO boss, Brand, and his ICO partner, Carter. ICO would contact Dax on his cell phone (which he never quite figured out how to work all the features on) when they needed him.

"Hey, Dax. Brand here. How's the weather?" This was their standard greeting to let Dax know he was being summoned.

"Well, it's cooling down some. We're putting in extra hours before winter hits us."

"Great, I'll check in with you later today. Bye."

Dax finished up the time cards for the day and told the crew he'd see them later.

From his truck, Dax called ICO back. Brand was on the another line, so he pulled out a cigarette and waited. Dax's company truck looked like a family of twelve was living inside. The front seat had a battered, hard leather briefcase that spewed all kinds of business forms, project plans, and time sheets from it. The rest of the seat and floor were covered with maps, blueprints, food wrappers, and empty cigarette packs. The smell was overwhelming! Not many people volunteered to ride with Dax because of the trash and the smell. Dax didn't really enjoy these surroundings either, but it kept most people away from him, which is what he wanted. The only item in Dax's truck that looked like it had a permanent place of its own was a silver cross that hung from the rearview mirror. When Mike from the day crew learned of his cancer, he gave Dax his cross. This made it very special to Dax.

Brand came on the line and said, "Hey, partner, how'd you like to go to Vegas?

"You going along?"

"Nope, this is just a dine and dash—a quick in and out."

"Okay, when do I leave?"

"How about now? Carter will pick you up in thirty minutes at the Wal-Mart by your place. Your bag is already packed."

An hour and a half later, when Dax was settled on the plane in passenger class, he opened his bag and pulled out this month's copy of Sports Illustrated. The cover had a picture of Tiger Woods with his broad grin and famous "gotcha" punch in the air. Dax loved playing golf. Asphalt Specialties sponsored a benefit tournament every year, and Dax was always there. He played every chance he got in the summer months. There ain't nothin' better than a good day of golfing, followed by drinking while talking about golfing.

Inside the magazine, there was a Polaroid picture of a man in his mid-fifties. He was tan, physically fit, wore expensive clothes, and had a noticeable silver chain necklace that held a cross at the end. There was no other information—no note, no instructions, no room key, no meeting place—just the picture. From working with Brand over the past ten years, Dax learned this picture represented either the "target" or the "protected." He never really knew which it was until he was in the situation.

Stepping into the Vegas terminal, Dax could feel the heat. The nonstop ringing of the slot machine bells and clanking of money in the trays could be heard as he approached the taxi stand. The next taxi in line scooped Dax up and sped out of the terminal. "Where to?"

"The Rio." Dax picked the Rio because it was off the beaten path of the strip. He hated crowds.

"This your first time to Vegas?"

"No, I come here about once a year. I don't know why I keep coming back. I always lose my ass."

"You want to know why you keep coming back? Well, let me ask you one question. What are you thinking' about when you're gambling? I'll tell you what you're thinking about. You're thinking about those sevens lining up. You're thinkin' about getting an ace for your first blackjack card, and you're thinkin' about winning a whole bunch of money! What you ain't thinkin' about is your job, your problems, your responsibilities—and that, sir, is why you keep comin' back to Vegas."

Dax smiled. He liked this guy and tipped him a fifty when he got out. He checked into the Rio, not knowing how long he would be there, under his partner's name, Carter Steele. He removed the contents of the bag ICO packed for him—one T-shirt, one dress shirt, one pair of socks, deodorant, toothpaste and toothbrush. This was going to be a quick trip. He brushed his teeth and opened the medicine cabinet mirror to put the toothpaste out of sight. Inside was a double action semi-automatic Smith & Wesson 45 loaded with a full ten-round clip, one in the chamber and a silencer on the barrel. Again, ICO knew his every move. Dax thought, if they know, then who else knows? This always bothered him. No one at ICO had crossed him yet, and he trusted Brand, so he kept his thoughts about his safety it to himself—for now.

Dax wanted a drink to wash down the desert, so he headed for the main bar in the Casino. The cocktail waitresses were very young and very nice to look at. Dax did his share of looking, but he didn't hit on them. That wasn't his style. Six rum and Cokes later, he strolled through the Casino past the maze of slots, past the poker tables, past the roulette wheel, and then he stopped. Sitting at the twenty-dollar-minimum blackjack table was the man from the picture. The clothes were different, but it was him—necklace and all.

Dax sat three chairs away from him and played several hands. The man had just lost six hands in a row and was getting a little pissy about it. Dax just played and watched, keeping one hand on the concealed .45. Behind the blackjack players was a row of dollar slot machines. They were called Dynamite Dollars. All five machines were being played by one man. The man had a system. He would put the maximum two coins in each machine, then return to the first machine. Next he pushed the PLAY MAX COINS button as fast as he could on all five machines. Then he looked at his watch and looked back up at the machines and watched them roll to their predetermined stop. Dax didn't really notice this routine when he first sat down, but he could tell by the piles of dollars in the trays that this guy had been playing them for some time.

The dealer's shift was over at this table, so the new dealer was setting up. As Dax watched the cards being shuffled, he noticed the man from the picture had turned his seat towards the slots. He looked at his watch and stared at the Dynamite machines. Dax followed the man's eyes and saw the first machine hit Dynamite! Dynamite! Dynamite! Then the second machine hit Dynamite! Dynamite! Dynamite! It was unbelievable that two machines had hit the progression within seconds of each other. Then the third, fourth, and fifth machines were lining up the same way.

The instant the last Dynamite lined up on the pay line, both the slot player and the man with the necklace bolted toward the rear of the casino. Dax didn't have time to think. He knew it was time to act. Dax hit the floor running, knocking down a few people as he ran. He looked over his shoulder and saw the new blackjack dealer running after him. Dax ran faster and faster. Thank God he was in such good shape! He hadn't drawn his gun yet, but when he hit the "employees only" door, he pulled out the .45 and slowed his pace.

The room was dark. He was in an area where rows of folding tables, chairs, plastic flower arrangements, dishes, and glassware were stored when not in use. He knew the two men he was chasing were in here. He could hear them breathing heavy. Less than half a minute later, the blackjack dealer burst through the door and shouted, "Ten seconds!" The next thing Dax heard was two shots being fired and the blackjack dealer's body hitting the floor.

Dax turned in the direction the shots were fired. Crawling on his hands and knees between the rows of tables, he listened for any movement. He got close enough to them to be able to hear them whispering. He thought he heard, "Who's the guy that ran after us?"

"I don't know. I thought maybe he was with you."

The next sound was an earsplitting explosion that sent everything in the room flying up to the ceiling and back down, crashing and shattering on top of all three of them. Dax was lifted off the floor and sent twenty feet across the room before his back hit the wall. He winced at the pain. He lay there quietly. He had no idea if the other two men had escaped or were injured and just laying low like he was. As if this weren't enough, the sprinkler system kicked in. Dax used this distraction to get up slowly up and look for the target. He saw the man he'd been sent there for with a broken plate embedded in his throat. The last thing he heard the man say was "Oh God." Dax leaned over him, checked his pulse, and closed his eyes.

The other man, the slot player, saw Dax approaching but did not move. His leg lay at a right angle to his body, broken. He couldn't move if he wanted to. "Please don't shoot, What do you want? Who are you?"

"Shut up," Dax demanded. "Your friend is dead, and you are alive. This is your lucky day." Dax walked back to the corpse and gently removed the cross necklace as proof of the man's demise. When he looked at the necklace, he hesitated. The cross itself was actually upside down on the chain. The horizontal bar was closer to the bottom of the vertical bar rather than the top. It was purposely made this way. Dax put it in his pocket and felt his way back to the door. The smoke and debris made it hard to breathe. People were running down the hallway, so Dax became part of the crowd making their way outside.

He walked until he was able to flag down a cab. He climbed in the cab. "Where to? Geez Mister. Are you alright? Do you want to go to the hospital?"

"No, just take me to the airport."

Dax cleaned himself up as best he could in the airport restroom. He proceeded to the ticket counter and bought his one-way ticket back to Denver. The red-eye flight from Denver just landed. Dax sat in the waiting area and watched the hopeful gamblers hurry by. His back was killing him. He stood up when he recognized his partner.

"Hey, Dax, you win big already?"

"Oh yeah, I won all right. I won another day to keep breathing." Carter smiled.

"You buy any souvenirs?"

"Here. this is the only thing that was worth shopping for." He handed Carter the silver cross.

"Great! I'm just here to clean up any messes you left behind. Have a good flight back." Dax boarded the plane, and after two drinks, slept the rest of the way home.

# CHAPTER 3

It was 2:00 AM when Dax got back to his apartment. His cell phone was ringing.

"Hi. I've been trying to call you all day."

"I've been busy." (This was Dax's pat answer for everything.) "It's late. I'll call you in the next couple of days, we are just real busy at work right now."

"You promise?"

"I'll call you. Bye." Before Dax fell asleep on the floor he thought about Peg. They met at the 92nd Street bar about six years ago. She was divorced with two children, which was something they had in common. He knew she loved him because she told him so.

Even though Dax's divorce had been several years ago now, he was still cautious when it came to anything close to a permanent relationship. He thought Nyckie loved him too, but that turned out bad. He had written a letter to his stepparents about why the divorce happened. He was raised in a Catholic family and needed to share his feelings with them about why he couldn't stay married. He regretted never mailing the letter. He took it out now and then and read it with a heaviness in his heart. His stepdad passed away last year, denying Dax the chance to explain why he had not stayed married to Nyckie.

The only two good things that came out of his marriage were his children. Dade, who turned fourteen on November 4 and Solei, who was eleven on November 27. Because of his job, he didn't get to see them very often and that bothered him a lot, but he talked to them on the phone to keep up on how they are doing. Last year, Dade wrote Dax a letter.

Dear Dad,

Mom and Solei and I went shopping today for stuff for school. I got some cool junk and some clothes. I know you work hard to send us money, and I know I wouldn't be having new things if it weren't for you. Next year I am going to try out for the wresting team, just like you did.

I miss you, Dad. When are you coming to visit again?

I love you,
Dade

Dax keeps this letter in his high school yearbook, where he keeps other private memories. Dade and Solei's pictures hang on his wall, and in his private moments, he talks to them and says "Good night" to each one before going to bed. His love for them runs deep.

Peg came into his life about two years after Nyckie and the children left. She sold real estate and tended bar. She was fun to be around. Everyone at the bar calls her Peg Bundy from the Married With Children TV show, only this Peg was prettier. Even though she is ten years older than Dax, she had a great body. She was a real people person, funny, witty—all the bar people like her. Dax could talk to her without feeling uncomfortable, and like most women who met Dax, Peg fell hard for him right away. He had the JFK Jr. charisma and warmth when it came to women. His thick, dark hair, wide, bright smile, and rugged physique are enough to make women look twice. But, it was his penetrating brown eyes that see to the core of a woman that made them fall in love with him.

When he was alone with Peg, he was totally there. He didn't think about anything or anyone else but her. As he was falling asleep tonight, he thought about the first night he and Peg had sex. She sat on his lap facing him, her legs tight in blue jeans spread out to fit around him. They both had had a few drinks and toasted a couple of shots of Wild Turkey, which they were feeling. She took her finger and traced his lips. His eyes were locked on hers. She was melting fast. "I want to kiss you," she whispered. He grinned. He knew what was coming next, but she didn't.

Dax leaned forward slowly until he could feel the heat of her lips—and then he stopped. When Peg moved forward to meet his kiss, he backed away ever so slightly. "You're teasing me," she begged.

"That teases me too," he responded. Then he gently nipped her lower lip a couple of times. "I bite."

"I see that." Their lips met several times—softly, lovingly. She wanted more. He wanted more.

His eyes searched her face slowly, looking for the satisfaction he hoped he was giving her. They both knew they would have sex that night. She followed him to his apartment. He had never taken a woman there before, but he didn't want to risk losing her that night. When they entered the door, Dax did not turn on the lights. He led her downstairs to where he slept on the floor. As Peg's eyes adjusted to the lack of light, she slipped into the bathroom.

"Are you all right?" Dax asked through the door.

"I'll be right out." When she opened the door, Dax was standing there in front of her—naked. Only the TV was on, which allowed her to see where she was going. Without hesitation, she removed her clothes. Her heart was racing now. The anticipation for both of them was more than they could stand. She joined Dax on the floor on top of a thick, soft comforter that lay in front of the TV. She had no clue what show was playing and didn't care.

The next few hours were filled with feeling him inside her over and over again. They couldn't stop the rapid physical movement they both experienced. As he lay on his back he told her to "turn around." She turned away from him and slid down on top of him—slowly at first and then faster, faster, faster, losing herself in the pleasure of the feeling.

"See, I'm not just a taker. You liked that, didn't you?"

"Yes, I did."

"I thought so." He smiled. He loved women, and he loved watching them in their moments of enjoyment, when surrendering to their physical needs.

They lay side by side, arms entwined and felt each other's hearts racing. He offered her a drink of water from a glass he had filled and set beside them on the coffee table. She took several drinks and lay back down. Now it was his turn. He rolled her over so she was lying on her stomach. When she realized what he wanted, she placed herself on her hands and knees and opened her body to him. She would not deny him anything.

But that was a few years ago now. Dax woke to the alarm at 5:00 AM. His hand was resting on his hardness. He thought of Peg as he eased the tension in his body. He showered and shaved quickly. He was tired and sore. On the way to the bridge site, he picked up some coffee and a newspaper. On page two was a short article about a big jackpot won in Vegas. It was pretty unusual to see anything about Vegas in the Denver paper, but since there were three gambling towns now in Colorado, news of a big jackpot traveled fast to spark the gambling community. The article simply said a man from California had won 30 million dollars on the Dynamite Dollars progressive and that the man planned to take all his relatives on a cruise. It appeared to Dax that his partner had done a fine job of cleaning up the mess Dax left behind. The real story behind the explosion would not be known by the public, but someday Dax would find out what it was all leading to.

Roger, Dax's boss, drove up in his company truck and said, "Hey, I need you to get some guys to the 120th and Federal site. They are getting ready to pour over there, and we need some guys to do the flatwork." And so another day on the job began. Dax visited four sites that day and made several trips to Tool King for replacement tools. The weather was getting colder now, so spending time in the truck was a luxury.

With the motor running, Dax looked over the sixty pages of prints for the bridge. He recalculated the metrics into feet and inches for the next phase of lining up the abutments at each end of the bridge where it would join the road. The crew didn't know how to work in metrics, so Dax did this for them. Math was easy for Dax, and so it was no big deal to him.

At JR's that night, he downed two shots of 101 just to get warm. A friend from the bar had gone to Sam's Club and bought Dax some thermal clothes for his Elk hunting trip next week, which he was looking forward to. It seems the women in Dax's life just wanted to take care of him, so he let them because he knew it made them feel good. He started letting his beard grow out now for the winter. The beard changed his looks dramatically, in a Jeremiah Johnson sort of way. This hunting week was a yearly family event. JR, his wife, sons, brother, nieces, and close friends, like Dax, took several campers and pulled them up to a site deep in the woods. The thing that Dax liked best about the whole week was the end of the day, sitting around the campfire telling stories and jokes. It just didn't get any better than that. Being far away from the city, no demands, no crises, and no wondering what bad things were going to happen next to good people. He spent a lot of time that week walking in the woods and thinking. He was thinking about his children, himself, and people who were now part of his life.

Waking up to a crisp, frosty morning, seeing his breath, filled him with peace. He relished the solitude, sitting in wait for the elk. ICO was far from his thoughts....

# CHAPTER 4

Winter passed slowly for Dax as far as work on the bridge was concerned. He and the highway department did not see eye to eye on things, so Dax took a voluntary leave of absence. During this time, he helped JR fix up the bar. They put up new walls, painted, recovered the chairs, painted the patio furniture, and put in new carpeting. The bar got a facelift and Dax managed to stay out of trouble there. Now it was spring, and that seemed to bring out the craziness in people for ICO. ICO was the kind of business where every day, every hour, every minute, events around the world dictated what was top priority. Brand had just come out of an all-night session with other heads of ICO from around the globe. They had used secure voice pattern combined with body language detection video conferencing to ensure they were talking to the real ICO employees. The combination of voice pattern intonations along with body language made it impossible to impersonate someone in this group.

Brand went to his office and covered his face with his hands. There were so many questions he needed to find answers to. Who was behind this? Whom could he trust? What would happen when they found what they were looking for? Brand had never let a case get to him, but this one was different. This one meant a change in belief for every man, woman, and child alive today. He locked his office and headed for home. He needed to be there now, close to his family, the people he cared about most.

Brand's wife of twenty-six years, Karen, had just put breakfast on the table for their three children. Jennifer, Curtis, and Ben were all four years apart in age. Jen was in high school and wanted to join the military when she graduated. Curtis was into junior high sports, and Ben was giving the teachers a run for their money in elementary school. Brand loved each one for their uniqueness. He took in this routine daily family breakfast with such an emotional impact, his eyes filled with tears. What he learned last night would destroy his family and all families like his unless he could find the answer and figure out what to do with the information when he finally had it.

After an hour nap, shower, and change of clothes, he went downstairs to where Karen was working. She ran her own sewing business from home. Having contracts with major sports teams made her very successful and kept her very busy. Brand was so proud of her and still very much in love. She worked hard at keeping her shape and looking nice for him. Every year she grew to love her husband more and more, if that was possible. So when he came into her office to kiss her good-bye for the day, she saw the worried look on his face.

"Is it as bad as all that?"

"I wish I could say it wasn't, but I can't. I love you, you know."

"I know." She smiled up at him and gently rubbed his forehead with her thumbs, trying to remove the worry.

"I'll be late again tonight, so don't wait to eat with me."

"Okay, the kids and I will miss you though."

"I'll call you when I get a minute."

They kissed and whispered their secret to each other—"Ways-a-Was." They said this each time they parted in person and on the phone. It meant, I love you the "way-it-was" the first time we made love.

Brand's 6'2" muscular frame filled his leather chair. He still worked out every day and kept sharp by sparring at the gym when he could. He didn't feel fifty, but there was no denying it. Everyone in his division of ICO was younger and stronger. He hated not being a part of the action anymore (but that was going to change).

He sat down to put in writing his plan for what would be the most secret and extensive assignment in his career. And so the list began:

1.  Pick a team that could be trusted inside ICO. (the fewer the better)
Team member criteria:
Highly skilled—no learning curve
Good knowledge of geographic areas involved
Be available for full-time assignment until completion
No interruptions of progress whatsoever
Will do as told, no questions asked
2.  Establish security inside and outside the team.
3.  Compartmentalize the project—KISS (Keep it simple...)
Assign who will do what and where.
4.  Keep informed.
5.  Answer the question, What do you do with the information once you have it?

Brand gave himself two hours to put his plan together; time was of the essence. The goal must be achieved before the information got into the wrong hands.

By 1:00 PM the day after he had been told about this crisis, he had contacted "the core team" and set up a meeting to detail (as much as they needed to know) the project and get things started. Around the table were Dax, Carter, Gage, Grant, and Brand. Gage Gunn had worked with Dax and Carter on other jobs where his "installation" skills for planting bugs, wiretaps, cameras, and such devices were key. If you needed something, anything installed, Gage was the man to get it there without being detected. Grant Stone (yes, his parents were having fun when they named him Granite Stone) was the logical, serious thinker of the group. So Brand had his team: Dax, the "get in there and do it" guy, Carter, the clean-up man, Gage, the installer, and Grant, the coordinator. Brand was pleased with his choices. He had trained them all himself and felt as close to them as he did his family.

"Good afternoon, gentlemen. It goes without saying that what we are about to discuss stays inside this room. For the past several years, the four of you have been involved in a variety of search, find, extinguish, or rescue operations. Many of these have been leading up to the assignment you are being given today. Because of the extreme urgency and importance, this mission has on the well being of the U.S. citizens, only the five of us will be 'activated' for this project. There may be other advance teams deployed to the cities where you will be sent. They will point you in the right direction and then you will be on your own. I, of course, will run things from here."

Dax, Carter, Grant, and Gage were attentive, but so far they hadn't heard anything new. Brand placed a large oak jewelry box on the table. It had a glass top and was lined in red velvet. As Brand slid the box closer to the men, they could see several crosses. Each cross was different in size, shape, color, material, and design. Each cross was embedded in the velvet as if a place had been made to fit each one perfectly. Some were more lavish than others. A five-inch red cross trimmed in silver resembled a stained glass cathedral window. Another, Byzantine-style, made of sterling silver and twenty-four karat gold, was in the center. This one had stones embedded in each arm and one in the center. The stones were said to have come from the regions where Christ walked. The names of the five cities where Christ preached were engraved on the cross as well.

Another cross that caught Brand's eye was a smaller one that was silver with a gold heart background. In the center of the cross was a smaller black heart surrounded by diamonds. This one looked a little familiar to Brand, but he couldn't place it at the moment. (It was one of the crosses burned onto the young girl's back from his first El Centro job with Brand.) Each cross had one thing in common. They were all made upside down. Dax recognized the cross from the man in Vegas and another one from a job he did in Denver over ten years ago. There were ten crosses in the box. The two remaining places were left waiting to be filled.

Brand stood silent for a few minutes as the men absorbed what they saw. "This project is called simply D.O.D., and your assignment is to bring back the last two crosses at all costs. There are other people looking for these crosses as well. I don't need to tell you that we can't let anyone else get to these before we do. We don't know who these people are. We just know they exist. And although we have secured these ten, it does us no good if we don't have the rest. You are to use whatever means necessary to secure the crosses and get them back here to me. You all know what you can control and what you can't, so remember to use your control to your advantage. I will be here if you need me.

"You have two hours before you leave. You must have a physical done by the ICO physician, pack a small suitcase, make your absence arrangements and be at the airport by 5:00 PM. You will be gone for however long it takes to complete the job. As usual, you will be given information when and where you need it. This is all for now. Good luck."

As the team was leaving the room, Brand called to Dax. "Dax, I need to ask you something."

"Sure, Brand. What's up?"

"I want you to think about your answer before you speak."

"This sounds serious."

"It is. If you knew the exact day you were going to die, would you do things different in your life? Would you change?"

"Well, I've never really thought about it before, but yeah, I probably would change."

Brand then asked, "Would you become a nicer person—not that you aren't a nice guy now—but would you spend more time with your family and friends, or would you have a live-for-today attitude and just do whatever the hell you wanted to do?"

Now Dax was getting concerned. "Brand, are you ill or dying?"

"N—no." Brand hesitated before looking Dax square in the eyes and saying, "Dax, we are all dying."

# CHAPTER 5

Dax caught up with Grant at the ICO hospital ward. "So, Grant. What do you think? Are we headed for trouble here?"

Grant was intimidating to everyone who didn't know him. He stood 6 foot 6 inches and had the body of an ironworker turned cowboy. His left arm displayed a tattoo of the US flag with an eagle flying through it that covered his entire forearm. Grant was used to people making jokes about how tall he was. Only a few people who really knew him knew that he had an IQ of 180 on a bad day. "Yeah, Dax. I'd say the old man picked us for a reason. He knows the more he tells us, the more we will drop our guard. This way, we are on full alert all the time." Just then the nurse arrived and called them both in. "See you on the other side!" Grant smiled back at Dax with a thumbs up.

Dax's physical went well. He was in top shape. The only treatment he got was the replacement of a clear contact in his left eye. Dax had gotten lasik surgery last year, compliments of ICO. The cornea flap in his left eye had not laid back down flat when it was replaced, so a soft contact was used as a precaution to keep it in place.

When Dax got home, his phone was ringing. "Hello."

"Hi, Dad."

"Hi, Dade. What's up?"

"My gym teacher says I have to have a new pair of tennis shoes."

"Okay, I'll wire you the money in half an hour."

"Great, thanks, Dad. Bye."

"Wait. How's school going?"

"Oh, okay, I guess. My gym teacher is also the wrestling coach. He's a really cool guy." Dax felt a twinge of pain because he wasn't there.

19

"That's good."

"Okay, My friends are waiting for me."

"Oh, okay. I'll talk to you later, bye."

"Bye."

By the time Carter, Dax, Grant, and Gage got to Denver International Airport, each had been contacted separately and told their destination. Dax and Grant were headed to Ocean City, Washington, on a flight to Seattle and then onto Aberdeen where they would rent a car to drive to Ocean City. After boarding the plane, they settled down to read their in-flight magazines. Both magazines coincidentally contained articles about Ocean City. A very small town located twenty miles north of Aberdeen on Hwy 109, the population was about fifty to seventy-five people with about 10,000 people showing up during razor clam season. Ocean City was famous for its razor clam beach. The seasons are from February 1 through July 15 and September 16 through December 31. They read all about how to dig for the clams and what the dos and don'ts were. Neither one had ever dug clams before, but there was a first time for everything! This adventure was beginning to appeal to Dax more and more. Since it was mid-June, the town would be crowded. Getting a room might be difficult, Grant thought to himself.

During the flight, they each received text messages on their pagers from Brand. They were to check into separate motels, which had already been booked, and get to know the locals. The town's people would lead them to the cross. That was right up Dax's alley. He could taste the rum and coke already!—that is, if there was a bar. When they set down in Seattle, they had to wait an hour for the flight to Aberdeen. Grant went for a walk because his tall frame had been cramped for two and one-half hours in coach. As he walked, he began noticing all the crosses people wore as accessories. It seemed like every other person was wearing a cross as a piece of jewelry somewhere on their body—necklaces, earrings, eyebrow rings, belt buckles, ankle bracelets, toe rings, shoe bobs, purse snaps. They were everywhere— not to mention the tattoos! When had he missed this fad? His brain started churning. Was the cross they were looking for on the way to Ocean City? And why Ocean City? Why not Seattle, where there were more opportunities to hide it? He kept his thoughts to himself and kept watching the people—his guard was up.

Dax headed for a phone to check messages at home. "Hi, Dad, it's Solei. I need a new pair of tennis shoes too! Love you, bye!" Gads, Dax thought to himself, those kids don't miss a trick. He found the money exchange and Western Union office and wired Solei the money. He also tried to call Peg at the bar, but she had taken the night off. He didn't leave a message nor did he try to reach her at home. He knew she wouldn't be happy about knowing he was going to be out of town for an indefinite period of time, so he just let it go.

They arrived in Aberdeen around 6:00 PM and grabbed a bite to eat. As they drove to Ocean City, they saw a lot of logging trucks coming from Hoquiam. According to the information they had read earlier, ITT Rayonier was a logging company that owned lots of land on the Olympic Peninsula. There were lots of other smaller camps and a few shake and shingle mills scattered throughout the area. It was after dark when they arrived in Ocean City, but Dax wanted to take a drive through town to get the lay of the land before going to the motel. It took all of ten minutes to get from one end of town to the other. Highway 109 was the main street. There was one other street with a few houses that ran parallel to the highway. The main street had seven motels, a real estate office, a grocery store, a souvenir shop, one bar and one bar/restaurant across the street from each other, one gas station/store/post office, a trailer park, and the junior high school for the whole school district. A left turn at the real estate office led you to the beach and the ocean, which was about a five-minute drive from town. That was pretty much it. Grant wanted to get checked in, so Dax dropped him off at the Sand Dollar Motel. They agreed to meet for breakfast around 9:00 AM.

Dax pulled into the Seven Seas Motel. It had five units, each with a kitchen (important to have during clam digging season), and three units with beds only. In the office, Dax rang the bell. It took a few minutes before a woman named Kay, or so her name tag read, who looked to be in her early thirties appeared from the back. "Can I help you?"

"Yes, do you have any rooms?"

"Yes and no. I have one room left, bedroom only, reserved for a guy named Carter Steele, but he hasn't shown up yet, so I guess you can have it." Since she seemed a little peeved about this Carter Steele guy, Dax decided not to tell her he was the Carter (once again using his partner's name for ICO while traveling) she was waiting for.

"Great! I'll take it."

"How long you plan on staying?"

"Well, I'm not sure yet. I might try the clamming and see how I like it. I've never done it before."

Kay gave him a look like she didn't quite believe him, but said, "Well, the first thing you'd better do is read this." She handed him a booklet on the rules to razor clam digging. "The Treasure House souvenir shop right across the lot there sells the licenses. They open at 5:00 AM. Here's the key to Unit 3. Can you pay in advance?"

"Sure." Dax paid for a week and turned to leave.

"If you need to use my kitchen for cleaning your clams, just let me know. I don't offer that to most people, but you seem like a nice enough guy."

"Okay, great! Thanks. Say, how late is the bar open down the street?"

Kay looked at her watch and said, "You got about an hour and a half. It closes at 2:00 AM."

Dax grabbed his suitcase from the car, turned the light on in his room, threw his suitcase on the bed, and out the door he went. It was a Wednesday, hump day, and the bar was pretty quiet. There were six men and two women sitting on the barstools, plus the barmaid. When Dax walked in, they all turned to see who it was. He had been here many times before—the unwelcome stranger. He took the next vacant stool, said "Hi" to the person next to him, and sat down.

"What'll ya have?"

"Rum and Coke with a twist of lime."

"Sorry, ran out of lime this morning. Get more tomorrow."

"That's fine." He sat quiet for a few minutes, which wasn't his nature, but since this was his first drink for the day, he didn't quite have the "Dax the wisecrack man" in him just yet.

"What brings you here to Ocean City?" the rough looking man asked him.

"Well, I thought I would try my hand at clam digging for a while and then just see what happens after that."

"Well, what do you know," the man said out loud to the rest of the usuals at the bar, "another clam digger! Guess somebody forgot to block the road off so people could just drive right into the ocean instead of polluting our town here. We sure as hell don't need another clam digger. You city folks just think you can come up here and play with our livelihood for fun to get a 'new experience' in your life. Clamming is this town's money, not yours. Why don't you just go back where you came from?"

Now everyone in the bar was looking at Dax. He decided this reception called for drastic measures. "Let me buy you a drink."

"Sure, but my buddies probably want a drink too."

"Set 'em up," Dax told the barmaid. She winked at the burly guy next to Dax and said, "Sure."

"I probably won't be here that long, just passing through."

"You staying at the Seven Seas?"

"Yeah, why?"

"You pay in advance?"

"Yeah, why?"

"Why? Because it's my wife that runs that motel, so now that I know that, you can stay as long as you like!" The big guy said, slapping his pal on the back. He turned back to his friends and Dax finished his drink.

"Good night," Dax said to no one in particular as he left the bar. When he shut the door, he heard the laughter.

"Bob, you got us that drink in record time! You still got the touch." Dax just smiled to himself as he walked back to his room. On the nightstand next to the bed was a handwritten note leaning up against the phone. It said, "Please call home when you get this. B."

Dax called Brand's office number and to his surprise, considering it was 2:45 AM, Brand answered. "Everything okay?"

"Brand what the h— are you doing at the office at this time of night?"

"Just couldn't sleep, I'm at home. I had my calls forwarded here in case you called."

Dax sighed. "Well, you can get some sleep now. We are all snuggled in for the night, safe and sound. You worry too much. Remember, you picked us because you trust us to come through for you, and we will."

"I know. It's just that this one, well, hits closer to home for me."

"Okay, I understand. I will check in more often if that will help."

"That would be good. Thanks, good night, Dax."

"Good night, and don't worry."

# CHAPTER 6

$T$he next morning, Dax was sitting in the restaurant reading the Daily World newspaper from Aberdeen since Ocean City did not have a paper of their own. Most of the news was about the local people wanting to stop the larger logging corporations from coming in and buying up all the smaller companies. Loggers in this part of the country were like the farmers of the midwest. Logging had been in their families for four generations, and they weren't about to give up without a fight.

"Morning. How'd you sleep?"

"Good." Grant pulled out a piece of paper with two lists. "I see you burned the midnight oil thinking again."

"Yep. I listed all the businesses on the North and South ends of town. I figured I would take the North and you the South. If we start visiting every place and talk to everyone in town, we should be outta here by Friday."

"Sounds good to me."

Dax took his list and put it in his shirt pocket. They ate breakfast and agreed to page each other if something turned up. Otherwise, they would see each other at the bar that night.

Grant left, taking the car, and Dax headed for the Treasure House Souvenir shop to get what he needed for clam digging. The shop was filled with everything imaginable made from seashells, clam shells, seaweed, sand, and driftwood. There were some one-of-a-kind treasures for sure, but no crosses that looked like what he was looking for.

"May I help you?" a woman from behind the counter said.

"Yes, I need a shovel for clam digging, a bucket, a license, and a pair of boots. That should do it."

24

"Well, I see you've come prepared," she said with a smile. "You can probably get by without the boots. Most people just roll up their pants and go barefoot, although the water is pretty cold this time of year. Maybe since you're new at this, you might want them."

"I think maybe I'll take the boots and see how it goes."

The woman put the items on the counter and in a kind way said,

"That comes to $56.25, including the license, which you don't need."

"Oh." He made a note that Kay had played a little trick on him. "Here you go."

Dax collected his new stuff, and on the way out the door turned back and with a wink, said, "Thanks for the free license!"

Standing on the beach ready to dig, Dax was thinking to himself, I look like I know what I'm doing, even if I don't. He pretended to dig while watching the people next to him. Eighteen clams being the limit, he figured he would really have to take his time, cause that didn't sound like a heck of a lot to him. The trick he was observing was that you really had to be quick. As the water washed back to the ocean, tiny holes or "shows" appeared when the clams withdrew their necks from the sand. Under those holes were the clams. Dax could see some people digging in and coming up with only one clam, while others came up with three or four in one scoop!

He tried a few digs on his own, but came up with either a broken shell or very small clam. He knew better than to toss them back. He read about the waste problem, as many as two million clams in one year had been destroyed this way. What he was after were the clams four to five inches long, that was where the good eaters were. After an hour, Dax had four very small clams and had not talked to anyone on the beach, so he stood back and watched the people. It was pretty easy to spot the tourists from the locals. The tourists looked like he did, clumsy and not much to show for their efforts.

Then he spotted Kay from the motel. She was bringing up clams with every shovelful of sand. Dax walked over. "Need some help?" he asked her.

Kay stood up straight and smiled. "Would that be help from you?"

"Well sure!"

She leaned over and looked in his bucket. "I see. I hope you weren't planning on eating these for your dinner?"

"Well, I was hoping to have enough to invite you to my place for a great meal."

"Here, give me your bucket." As Kay proceeded to dig clams for Dax, he started his investigation by asking her a few questions.

"So, how long have you and your husband been running the motel?"

"Bob doesn't run the motel. I do. Going on three years ."

"You must know everyone in the town by now."

"This one and the next in all directions. Are you looking for someone?"

Since he didn't want to arouse suspicion, Dax said, "No, not really. I just like learning about people and how they live in different parts of our country."

"You write about them or something?"

"Well, I do keep a journal, but it's really just for me." Kay finished filling Dax's bucket with the limit allowed.

"Here you go. I gotta go do some things, but if you would like to stop by the office later, I'll give you a cooking lesson and show you the right way to eat these things."

"Great! See you later then." He made a mental note to himself that he would have to be careful with Kay. Her husband was a big logger, and Dax wanted no part of that.

Meanwhile, at the other end of town, Grant decided to use his "My-dog-jumped-out-of-the-car. Have-you-seen-him?" routine. He actually had a picture of his dog with him.

He knocked on the first door, and a woman in her mid-twenties answered. She didn't unlock the outside door, and there were two small children peeking out from behind her.

"Hi, sorry to bother you. My family and I are on vacation. We stopped for lunch down the street, and our dog jumped out of the car. I was wondering if you happened to see a strange dog around? Here is his picture."

She looked at the picture through the screen door and said, "No, I haven't seen this dog. Sorry." And with that, she shut the door before Grant had a chance to say another word.

"Geez, I must be losing my touch," he said out loud to himself. At the next house, there were two boys playing catch outside. Grant said, "Hey boys, I'm looking for my dog. Here's his picture. have you seen him?"

The boys ran over and looked at the picture. The older boy said, "You giving a reward for finding him?"

"Sure twenty bucks each if you find him. I'll come by later and see if you had any luck. Say, is your mom or dad home?"

"No, just our grandma, and she's napping, so I wouldn't bother her if I were you." With that, the boys ran off in search of the nonexistent dog. Well, at least that would keep them busy for awhile, Grant thought.

Okay, two strikes, now he needed to hit pay dirt. He decided to try the other motel he had not checked into. He rang the bell at the desk. An older guy came out from the back. "Can I help you?"

"Yes, do you have any rooms?"

"I guess you didn't see the No Vacancy sign out front."

"Oh sorry. No I didn't. Do you know if any of the other motels have vacancies?"

"Nope. How long you gonna be here?"

"Well two days, at least. I've never been this far north. I had no idea everything would be so green. It is pretty scenic here."

"Well, if you want, I can call the four other motels and see what they got. That will save you the trouble of driving up and down the street."

"That would be great—thanks."

Grant listened. "Hey, Lorraine, Gus here. How's your mom? Uh-huh, well, they get pretty uppity when they think they know more than the doctor. You just gotta pamper them once in a while. Say, I got a guy here who's lookin' for a room. You got any vacancies? Okay, I'll tell him. Thanks. Say 'hi' to your mom for me. Bye." He turned to Grant. "Nothing there. I'll try another."

"Thanks. " You don't have to go this trouble."

"Ain't no trouble. Gives me a chance to catch up with my neighbors anyway." After all four motels were called with no vacancies, Grant asked Gus how long he had been running this place. "I guess going on twenty-two years now, but not always just doing this. I used to run the newspaper over in Aberdeen, but then my eyesight started going, so this is where I have been ever since."

"So do you have much excitement around here or does everyone get along pretty good?"

Gus walked around the counter and made himself comfy in one of two chairs in the lobby. "Well, mostly it's quiet here, except on Friday or Saturday nights when the loggers come in from camp to toss back a few. Then they might tear things up a bit, but usually nothing serious. How long did you say you were planning on staying?"

"Oh, just a couple of days."

"Well, if you are still here on Friday night, I would steer clear of the bar at the end of town. That's where they usually go."

"Okay, I'll keep that in mind." Grant got up to leave and turned back to say. "I'm kind of a collector of an antiques. Are there any places around here where I might find some treasures?"

Gus gave a short laugh. "The only thing old around here you might be interested in would be at the store across from the Seven Seas. The lady that runs that place keeps some pretty weird stuff."

"Okay, thanks for the tip. I'll let you know if I find anything."

Grant walked a few more blocks down to the real estate office. He read the ads for the few houses that were for sale in Ocean City and the surrounding areas. None of them looked too inviting. He went in and asked about a couple of the houses and found out most of them had been abandoned by families that got tired of working in the logging camps seven days a week and still couldn't make a decent living. He could not even imagine such a life. The realtor told Grant that most people didn't stay too long unless they had a business of their own. He mentioned the store across from the Seven Seas because that lady was the oldest person in town, and she wasn't going anywhere. "Why, she hardly comes out of her house behind the store. Funny lady" he said, shaking his head.

Grant took a couple of flyers and said "Think I'll just go walk by a couple of these. Thanks." Now that he had heard about this store for the second time today, he would definitely have to pay this lady a visit. But it was almost time to meet Dax, so he headed for the restaurant/bar.

Dax of course, was in the bar, having his third rum and Coke when Grant arrived. "Well, how was your day?" Grant asked as he ordered a Bud. " Or did you spend most of it in here?"

"I'll have you know I dug a whole bucket full of clams for our dinner tonight."

"Thanks, but I'll pass. They're all yours. Did you dig up any crosses while you were on the beach?" "Not a one, but I did get an invite to dinner with the gal who runs the Seven Seas motel. I plan to see what she can tell me about this place and where in the heck we might find what we are looking for."

Grant set his glass down and said, "Yeah, well, twice today people told me about this old gal who runs the store across the street from your motel lady, so I was planning on checking that out tomorrow."

"Alright then. Sounds like we both have a plan."

# CHAPTER 7

Back in Denver, the weather had been exceptionally hot already and summer had not even officially started. Brand was spending a lot of time at the office and not much time with Karen and the kids. Karen could tell he needed a break. For the first time in two weeks, the whole family was at the dinner table. They had gone to 8:00 AM Sunday Mass as usual, but then each went their separate ways for the day. The boys went to baseball practice, and Jennifer went to the mall with friends. Karen was in the yard planting flowers, and Brand was at his computer in his office.

Dinner was good, and everyone had lots to say about what they wanted to do this summer for vacation. Since Jenn would be graduating from high school this year and going away to school somewhere, they were excited about planning a family vacation.

"How about we go to Hawaii?" Ben asked. "We could get a motel on the beach, go surfing, snorkeling, and take one of those kite rides from the back of a boat! That would be awesome."

Karen looked at Brand until he looked up at Ben. Brand said, "That sounds great to me, but is that what everyone else wants to do?"

"Yeah! Yeah! Yeah!"

Brand smiled at Karen, "Well?" Karen was thrilled!

"Hawaii, are you kidding? I can't believe you said we would go—just like that!"

"You only live once, and you can't take it with you, so let's do it." Then his smile went away. "The only problem is, it will have to wait until this assignment is over—should be no more than two weeks." The kids were excited and after clearing the table ran to call their friends.

"Brand, I don't think you are going to last another two weeks. You have been at the office practically day and night. We haven't had any 'alone' time for days."

"I know. I'm sorry, but you know I wouldn't be there if I didn't have to be."

Karen came over and sat on Brand's lap. "How about if this week-end you and I hop on the Harley and go to Crested Butte for a couple of days? You can take your laptop, pager, cell phone, and work from there if you have to? Please?"

Knowing what he knew about his wife, she never asked for something unless she really, really wanted it. How could he resist? Just having her sit on his lap and run her fingers through his hair was enough to make him relax and think about making love to her.

"Okay, but I might have to work a little while we are there, you know."

"I know. Guess I'll just have to go shopping then!" She got up with a smile on her face.

Friday could not come fast enough for Karen. She made all the pick-up plans for the kids activities and put food in the frig. Of course, ordering pizza was always the number one thing they did when the "old folks" were gone. Brand got home around 10:00 PM that night exhausted. He ate a bit of leftover lasagna and went to bed. Knowing that they were leaving in the morning, he was excited but apprehensive at the same time.

The alarm went off at 5:00 AM. Brand had already slept an hour more than he normally did. He felt great. Karen had the Harley bags packed with just enough of everything for three days. One day to get down there, one day there, and one day to get back. This had become an annual trip about four years ago, when they just happened to take a ride and ended up in Crested Butte on the fourth of July. There were live bands that played outside and people danced in the street. They loved the small town that was dwarfed by Mt. Crested Butte. She had packed so many times for bike rides, it only took her half an hour the night before. No rain suits though, they would chance it. Karen had been riding on the back of Brand's bikes since she was fifteen and he was seventeen, and she always looked forward to every ride. Talk about feeling free and being a part of nature. There was nothing like it.

Crested Butte would be an all day ride, about eight hours, so they would be stopping for breakfast and maybe lunch on the way. "Okay, daylight's wasting." Brand always said this as they climbed on the bike. He bought this new bike two summers ago. He couldn't believe he had it this long already. He only had 2,000 miles on it, which told him he definitely needed to ride more. It was a deep red Road King, loaded with hard bags on the sides and back, plus several mini-compartments for "stuff." It came with a CD player, CB radio, front and rear speakers, reverse, and air shocks. He had added some chrome—a must for all Harley riders—and kept it clean and covered inside the garage.

They headed out on I-25 south, not much traffic this early on a Saturday. Then they got on 285 south and cut over on 67 South towards Deckers. The Deckers-Pine area had had a bad forest fire three years ago, and the charred trees told the story as they rode by. This road was one just made for a motorcycle. It twisted and turned through the pine trees with mountains on both sides. It was one of their favorites.

The restaurant they stopped at for lunch the first time they had gone this way was open, so they decided to stop for breakfast. It was a new log cabin type building. The food was all homemade, and the people working there made sure everything was top notch. After eating and heading back down the road, Brand started enjoying the trip. They wouldn't stop now for a few hours, when they needed gas. The sun was starting to rise and warm them up. Seeing the sunrise was one of nature's presents that Brand appreciated. As they rode, Karen would point out any wildlife or unusual sites, so they could share the moment.

About 11:00 AM they pulled over to take off their chaps and jackets and to get an ice cream cone from the country store. Brand took this chance to check his messages. "Hey, Brand, just checking in. Grant and I are cruising the town and hope to have something for you tomorrow. We haven't seen anything of Gage or Carter, so I'm not sure what they're up to. I'll call you tomorrow about noon, later."

I-24 west runs along the Arkansas river west to Gunnison. Karen was enjoying every minute. The sun was beating down on them now, and it was quite warm. Her mind was wandering. She had already thought about the kids, her work, her relatives, life in general, new things she wanted to do, and her life with Brand. When they went on road trips, Karen would wear the sexy Harley tops Brand liked. She looked very good and was glad of it. Her desire for sex had increased in the last couple of months. She wasn't exactly sure why this was, but thought maybe it had something to do with the exercise class she started. She had more energy than ever, and she could see the results. Whatever the reason, she was now thinking about different places to have sex with Brand. She had made a secret "fantasy" list in her head of all the places she wanted to do it with him.

Brand had put in a Michael Bolton tape. "When a Man Loves a Woman" was playing loud and clear as they went down the road. He could feel Karen moving around on the back, which was unusual because most of the time he couldn't even tell she was behind him. He felt two places of warm soft skin on his back. He wondered what that was, but didn't move his body at all. It took about five seconds for him to recognize what he was feeling. All men know this feeling. It is the unique sensation you get when you feel a woman's breast. He could not believe it! What was she doing back there? He didn't turn around, but sat up a little straighter, which brought a smile to Karen's face. She knew she had surprised him.

Then she ever so slightly rubbed her nipples on Brand's back. This got her really excited and Brand was getting hard. Brand started looking for a place to pull over. There was a turn out up ahead. He slowed down and parked. Karen gave him a big smile. "Let's take a hike up there." He pointed to a small cliff. He grabbed their jackets and up they climbed into the trees.

They found a small clearing among the pine trees. Brand spread the jackets down on the ground. They both began undressing each other. They kissed every place a piece of clothing was removed. Karen laid down on the jackets. The sun was warming her entire body.

Brand straddled her, smiling. "You look like you really are enjoying this."

"I am!"

Brand took his index fingers and ever so lightly made small circles on the very tips of Karen's breasts. She loved this, and he knew it. The slower he did it, the more she moaned. She felt the warm pull of her desire between her legs. Brand rubbed her gently down there.

Then Karen traded places with Brand. He was still very much ready for whatever she wanted to do. Karen knew what Brand liked too. She felt his hardness between her legs. They were lost in each other. The fact that they were doing this outside, in the mountains, seemed to heighten their senses. The idea of being a little naughty and the excitement of not getting caught made them feel like teenagers again. They kissed very passionately after-wards and lay there for just a minute longer. Karen wanted to remember this for a long time. They got dressed and started down the mountain. Karen picked up a rock.

Brand asked, "What are you doing?"

"I'm getting a souvenir. This is a moment to remember, don't you think?"

"Definitely. You are just full of surprises, aren't you?"

As Karen climbed back on the bike, she said, "Yes, I am, and there is more where that came from good lookin'!"

The rest of the ride was great. They couldn't have asked for better weather, no rain, with a few clouds now and then to cool them down. They got to Gunnison about 3:00 PM. All they had left was twenty-four miles up Hwy 135, and they would be there. They pulled into the Sheraton on Gothic Road, which was located at the bottom of the mountain. There are no green runs, only blue, black, and double diamonds for the skiers that liked to live on the edge.

The town of Crested Butte itself was in the valley below the mountain. The main street was Elk Avenue. It was about eight blocks long. In this strip were several T-shirt/souvenir shops, restaurants, jewelry stores, and a cou-ple of bars. This was definitely a small mountain community. The people here were very proud of their community and culture. The population as of

2000 was 1,616. The average age was 34. Both Crested Butte and Mt. Crested Butte are known for their many cultural events. They boast to be "Colorado's Wildflower Capital." Most of the landscape was left to the elements for wild flower growth and mountain views. The residence in both towns range from the "back to nature" to the very rich, which creates quite a variety for the people watchers sitting on the town benches for entertainment. You can buy everything from a picture frame made from wildflowers to a pair of leather pants for $900!

Summer events include holistic health fairs, art auctions, hot air balloon festival, ballet performances, poetry readings, and world-renowned orchestra concerts. Most people came here in the summer for the hiking, biking, and golfing.

Brand and Karen checked in and got settled. Brand checked his messages. He had two, both marked urgent. "Brand, this is Chad at the ICO hotline. Thought you should know, we have lost our visual on Dax. One minute he was in a bar and the next, the screen went black. If you need us to send someone to him, let us know. Bye." Brand did not like hearing that, but wasn't too worried just yet. "Brand, Dax here. It's Saturday morning about 2:00 AM. I'm afraid I have a little bad news. Gage is in the hospital, but he's gonna be okay. Here's the short story. Gage and Carter showed up at the logger bar here in town Friday night with the rest of the crew. Seems a kid got killed in an accident at the logging site. Gage said the wrong thing to the wrong guy at the bar, and it turned into a brawl. The doctor said he has a concussion, collapsed lung, broken arm, couple of cracked ribs, and some bad bruises. They are going to keep him for a day or two and then he'll be coming home. I'll give you more details when I talk to you. Don't worry, the rest of us are good. Talk to you tomorrow." While Brand did not like hearing that either, it probably explained why they lost Dax on visual. He undoubtedly got punched in the eye.

From the look on Brand's face, Karen knew the news was not good. She didn't ask, and Brand didn't tell. He only said he would have to make some phone calls later. The city bus took people who stayed in Mt. Crested Butte down to Crested Butte and vice versa on a regular schedule. Brand and Karen thought they would go to town, have a few drinks and dinner, and call it a day. They planned to spend most of their time by the pool tomorrow—if all was well with work.

To a visitor, Crested Butte looks like a small laid-back town with not much happening, but it also has its mysteries. The story Vanished that aired on ABC was about Neil Murdoch who was a teacher in Crested Butte for twenty-five years. He was the "Godfather of the Mountain Bike" until he disappeared in 1998. He was wanted by the police for charges related to drug smuggling. The federal agent who tried getting information about Murdoch did not find the citizens of Crested Butte very cooperative. No one wanted to help him get captured. So, no one talked to the authorities. However, despite the town's unwillingness to talk, Murdoch was captured and went to trial. Neil was the talk of the town for many years.

There were over thirty restaurants within the eight by six block business district, but Brand and Karen had their favorites. First they took the stairs up to the Eldo bar, "A Sunny Place for Shady People," for a couple of drinks. They were sitting out on the balcony that overlooks the streets when all of a sudden they saw a cowboy riding a bull up the street!

"Look at that!" Karen pointed. "Now that's one way to get where you're going, I guess." The cowboy sure got lots of attention, and then he did something even crazier! He walked the bull right into the Idle Spur Grill and Brewery.

"Guess he is going to dinner, Crested Butte style," Karen said as the bull disappeared into the restaurant.

The construction workers were starting to stroll in for happy hour at the Eldo. Condos on the mountain and top dollar homes around the country club were in demand. This was definitely the younger crowd bar, and Brand and Karen enjoyed hearing their stories. They stayed for about an hour and then headed for dinner. By the time they reached the Idle Spur, the bull and its rider were gone, but people were still talking about it.

"That Charlie is crazy. Good thing he knows the owner or he would have been in a lot of trouble," said the bartender with a wink.

While the town was small and not noted for celebrity sightings, it had it moments. The Idle Spur restaurant/bar was partly owned by the actor Tom Skerritt. Tom was best known in Hollywood for parts in Top Gun, War Hunt, Path to War, and A River Runs Through It. Tom's daughter and son-in-law, Erin and Randy, managed the place. The Idle Spur was home of the Crested Butte brewery. Their flagship beer was called Red Lady Ale, named after the Red Lady bowl on top of Mt. Emmons, which overlooks the town. Most fourth of July's, Tom and his wife come to town to visit the kids. They spend a good amount of time strolling the town, visiting with the locals who know him by his first name and can be seen sitting on one of the metal sculpted benches on Elk Avenue, taking in the sites.

"What's good tonight?" Brand asked the waiter.

"Everything, but the steak is real good right now."

"Okay, we'll take two filets, medium well, baked potato with the works, and two dinner salads with ranch."

"Great, I'll bring your drinks and salad right out."

Dinner was great and Karen and Brand decided to walk down the street and browse to walk off their full stomachs.

There were always new shops every year they visited. Karen found a pair of earrings and a motorcycle charm for a necklace that she really liked.

"Which one should I get? The earrings or the charm?" she asked Brand.

34

He said "Get both," as he handed her the money to pay for both things. He sure knew how to spoil her, she thought to herself. But she knew Brand liked buying things for her when she picked them out. He always had a hard time when it came to shopping for her.

# CHAPTER 8

Dax walked into the bar Friday night about 5:00 PM. Grant walked in a little after 6:00 PM.

"Hey."

"Hey" was their normal greeting to each other. Grant was not happy. "That old gal over at the store wouldn't even come outside to talk to me. I tried everything I could think of to get her to talk about herself, her family, anything, but she just said if I wasn't buying anything, then I could just move along. I even tried buying something, but she was onto me and said the store was closed."

Dax grinned, "Boy, you are losing your touch, aren't you? I'll see what Kay can tell me about her tomorrow."

With one eyebrow raised, Grant said, "You aren't getting involved with this Kay gal, are you?"

Dax shot back, "You of all people should know better than that. Strictly business when on business. I don't need or want any baggage in my life."

All of a sudden, the front door burst open and about twelve loggers piled in. They were dirty, sweaty, and all talking about the accident.

"How in the H— did that happen anyway? Who was supposed to be watching the kid?" one of the older men asked.

When Dax and Grant turned around, they spotted Gage and Carter among the twelve men. They looked like they hadn't showered or shaved for a week! All four men's eyes met, but they did not talk to each other. That would come later.

"So that's where those two have been hiding," Dax spoke softly to Grant.

"Better them than us," Grant added.

The old logger said the kid's name was Tim. Tim was new and did the job of a bucker which meant that after the feller made the tree fall, Tim would walk out onto the tree and cut it into specific lengths. Somehow, another tree must have come loose when the first one fell. When Tim walked out onto the log, the other tree hit him in the back. He was killed instantly.

Shots and toasts went all night for Tim. The crews were a pretty tight group and took it hard when one of them got hurt or killed.

Gage said, "Well it's a bad deal all the way around, but the kid should have known to check the other trees around him before he walked out on that log."

That was all it took. The next thing Gage knew, he was looking up from the floor at a huge logger who had just decked him. As the guy picked Gage up off the floor, Gage hit him with all his weight in the stomach. The man didn't flinch. Gage was thrown down hard on a table. It shattered, and all hell broke loose.

It was every man for himself now. Dax and Grant turned around on their seats at the bar. They watched as their partner was being tossed around like a paper cup going down some rapids. Carter had already joined the brawl, trying to keep whoever he could off Gage. Dax and Grant could only take so much. They came off their barstools and joined the brawl. They were met with six guys who looked like they would love to beat the crap out of them, which they did. This was definitely not what Dax had in mind for the evening. Dax would much rather walk away than physically fight with someone, but this time there was no choice.

After what seemed like an hour of flying fists, bottles, and people, one of the loggers shouted, "Let's get the hell out of here before the sheriff throws our asses in jail again!" With that, the ten men left for who knows where. They each gave Gage a kick as they went out the door. He was unconscious.

"Can you call an ambulance?" Dax asked.

"One's on the way," the bartender said.

Dax picked Gage's head up and rested it on his lap. He got some ice and put it on his eyes, which were badly swelling. Gage came to slightly, but had no clue where he was.

Carter shoved Dax aside and took over. "Thanks, buddy, but we take care of our own around here."

"Sorry, I was just trying to help."

The ambulance took thirty minutes to get there. The paramedics checked Gage's vital signs, put in an IV in him, placed an oxygen mask on his face, and lifted him on the cart. Carter rode in the back of the ambulance to the hospital.

"Where will they take that guy?" Dax asked as he limped back to the bar stool. Dax's nose bleeding, and he was walking with a limp.

"They'll take him over to Aberdeen, and if he's real bad they might fly him over to Olympia. You don't look so hot either. You should probably have that leg looked at."

"I'll be okay." Grant had landed more punches than he took, so he didn't even look like he had been in the middle of things. Size does have its advantages.

Dax winced as he lifted his glass, "I think I'll call it a night. See you tomorrow for breakfast."

Grant noticed Dax's face, "You sure you're gonna be okay? You want me to find the local doctor?"

"No, I just need to take a couple aspirin and call myself in the morning. See you tomorrow."

"Okay, about 9:00? You might want to sleep in."

"Okay, night."

Dax had a fitful night of sleep. His whole body ached, and he had bruises everywhere. He got up about 8:00 AM and decided he would ask Kay where the local doctor's. office was so he could get some painkillers. Posted on the office door was a note: "Over at Ina's. Be back in an hour."

Ina was the old lady Grant had been trying to get to talk to, so Dax limped across the street and knocked on the door to what looked like the living quarters next to the store. Kay answered the door. She looked Dax up and down.

"I see you met the logging crew last night. Nice bunch of fellas, aren't they? Are you in pain?"

"Yeah, you could say that."

"Well, come in and sit down. I'm sure Ina has something that will make you feel better."

"Thanks."

An elderly lady was lying on the couch. "Ina, this is Dax. He's staying at the motel for a couple of days. He got caught up in the Friday night fun at the bar and looks like he lost the fight." Ina did not turn in Dax's direction.

"Hello, Dax. So our local boys showed you their best side, did they?"

"Well, if that is their best side, Ma'am, I sure don't want to see their worst side."

"You can call me Ina." Ina pointed to the kitchen. "Kay, in the cupboard by the stove, you should find some 222's to help Dax here with his pain."

Dax looked around the room. It was dark and full of old furniture and newspapers, and it looked like things had not been dusted in a while.

Kay came back from the kitchen. "Here, take a couple of these every four hours until you feel human again, and sit down before you fall down."

"Thanks." Dax took two pills and sat in an old green stuffed chair that looked like it was made from old drapery material and pinewood.

Kay picked up the newspaper and started to read it out loud to Ina. Dax had not noticed Ina was blind.

38

"It says here the clamming season this year has been the best yet. The marine biologists say this is due to the ocean temperature heating up, and that makes the clams more active during mating season." Kay continued reading for another fifteen minutes and put down the paper.

Dax looked around the room and saw a lot of mostly junk with stacks of stuff piled on top of each other. There were a couple of pictures of three women standing in front of a gas station. One of the women looked like a young version of Ina. There was also a book on a stand that was open with a bookmark in it. Dax guessed that Kay must also read books to Ina.

Kay put down the paper. "Ina, I wrote the checks for your bills so I'll put those in the mail today. Is there anything special you want for lunch? I can come back after I clean the rooms." Ina still did not move from the couch. She held her arm up to touch Kay.

"No, I can get my own lunch today, dear."

Kay gave a wink to Dax and said back to Ina, "You want Dax here to take you for a walk outside?"

"Now why would I want to go outside? I didn't leave anything out there?"

Kay smiled at Dax. "Okay, just thought I would check. I'll be back later this afternoon then."

"Nice to meet you Ina, Hope I didn't disturb you by coming over here," Dax said.

"No, young man, you didn't. It's kind of nice to hear a different voice. If you are staying around, you can come back and visit and tell me about yourself. That way I'll have some new gossip to share with Kay."

"Okay, I just might do that. Bye."

# CHAPTER 9

$K$ay and Dax walked back across the street. It was time for Dax to meet up with Grant.

"Say, Kay, she sure is an interesting old lady. How long has she lived here?"

"She's been here since the early 1940's. She has led a very interesting life. She's from Kansas originally and lived in Anacortes, Washington, when she was little. She quit school when she was fourteen to do housecleaning for money. Later, she and her sister worked fish traps, cannery, and clamming in Alaska. She went back to Anacortes and became a foreman in a cannery in Taholah. She has told me stories about her digging up over 100 pounds of clams daily and then canning them at night. Talk about a workhorse! She also did some teaching on the side for the Taholah Indian Tribe.

"She was married for a short time, but if you ask her about him, all she will say was 'He thought he was a gambler.' So, my guess is she left him since she didn't need him to support her.

"She started working for Mrs. Davis at the store when she came to Ocean City, and she ended up becoming the post mistress. That is how she knows so much about everybody in town without going out of her house. She bought the old Gun Club and opened Nina's Mercantile with gas pumps and the post office. Her father and brother built the two bedroom house she lives in now that's attached to the store.

"She was the kind of person who would give a family credit when things got tough, cause she knew what that was like. Her only rule was that they couldn't charge liquor or cigarettes. During the war, she helped servicemen get home when they were on furloughs by buying them a ticket. She wrote to a lot of the servicemen and kept everyone in town updated on where they were. She really cares about the people and the town. They are just as much her family as her real family."

"She sounds like a quite a gal," Dax commented.

"The town is grateful she came and stayed. There's more to her than meets the eye. Well, gotta get busy now. See you later."

"Okay, see you later."

When Dax got to the restaurant, Grant had already eaten. "You get lost or what?"

"No, I met the infamous Ina you've been trying to get close to. She even invited me to come back."

With a broad grin Grant said, "As usual, you always get the women. Did you find out anything that will help us?"

"Not yet, but I'm going back later. I have a hunch this is the one." They talked some more, and Grant decided he would head over to check on Gage. He would call Dax later and see if he needed to come back to Ocean City or just head on home. Dax had more than a hunch Nina was the key, so he told Grant to go ahead and head for home, but to call him later just in case. Dax ate some lunch and went back to the motel.

When he woke up it was still light outside. He had slept for about two hours and felt worse than when he lay down. He took a couple of Ina's pills and headed for the bar. It was early evening on a Saturday night, so there weren't too many people in the bar. This time, the bartender had Dax's drink waiting for him as he eased himself onto the stool.

"Thanks."

"I saw you comin' across the lot. You look like you're still hurtin' from last night."

"You could say that." Dax took a long drink and said, "So, I guess last night was sort of routine around here. Or do they just get like that when there's been an accident?"

"Well, most times, these boys are pretty good, but now and again they just need to blow off steam. Last night was a bad one because of the boy getting killed. Any one of them would give you the shirt off their back, if you asked 'em."

"Have you heard anything about the guy they took in the ambulance?"

"Yeah, Ina called up there this morning, and they said he will be okay, but won't be workin' for a while. Guess he'll be going back to wherever he came from to heal up. He hasn't been with that crew very long either."

Even though Dax knew who Ina was, he asked anyway "Who is Ina?"

"Oh, she's the gal that runs the store across the street and down a bit. She keeps tabs on everyone in town and let's everybody know what's going on. She can't see, but that don't stop her from keeping up with things around here. A nice old gal."

Dax didn't know if he should push his luck and ask more questions about Ina, but he thought maybe one more wouldn't hurt.

"Does this Ina keep up with things going on outside of the town too?"

"Oh yeah, she's a real Seattle Rainiers baseball fan and has an autographed ball from the 1949 team. She's been on the school board. She organized the local election board. She even got the road paved and a bridge built for the town so people didn't have to wait for the tide to go out to get into town. She's been a real asset to the town. You won't find anyone who will talk bad about Ina. We all love her."

"Sounds like every town could use a person like her."

"Yep." Dax said to himself "Bingo. Ina is 'the one.'"

It was going on 5:00 PM now, so Dax decided he would go back to Ina's. She had to be the key.

Dax knocked on the door. "Who's there? If I know ya, come on in. If I don't, then go away."

Dax chuckled, "Well, we just met this morning, so I guess you could say you know me now. It's Dax."

"Oh, come on in. Don't make me yell out the darn door anymore."

"Hi, Ina. Is now a good time for me to visit? I'll probably be heading out tomorrow."

"Sure, I ain't doin' nothing." Dax sat in the chair beside the couch. There was a tray table in front of the couch with soup and crackers on it, Ina's dinner he guessed.

"So, the folks around this town speak pretty highly of you. Seems like you have done a lot for these people."

"Well, I've done some things, but nothing anybody else couldn't do. I just did it first, that's all."

"Do you have family around here?"

"No, my parents, brothers, and sisters are all deceased. All buried up in Anacortes. I'm the last one. Guess I'm too ornery to let go just yet. I get the feeling there's something else I'm supposed to do, but I don't know what that could be. Anyway, enough about me, what's your story, Dax?"

"Well, there's really not much to tell. I come from a large family of twelve kids, some half-sisters and brother. My real mother was put in a hospital because her mind didn't work quite right. My real dad liked alcohol a little too much, so we were raised by my stepmom and dad. Dad passed away, and Mom is still in the Chicago area. I went back to visit her not too long ago. She's a real trooper. I don't keep in contact with my brothers and sisters. We all kinda went our own way."

Ina asked, "You married?"

"Not now. Was once, but that didn't turn out too good. I've got two real good kids from it, so it wasn't all bad. I don't see them as much as I should, but I do the best I can."

"Well, Dax, family is important, but so are friends, and if you are lucky enough to have both, then you've done alright. As long as you do the best you can while you are here, that's what counts. In the end, everybody dies alone. You don't take anybody with you when you go, you just go. But the thing to remember while you are here is that even after you are gone, people will remember the kind of person you were—good or bad, they remember."

"Okay, Dax, you seem like a good person, what little I know now. I'm kind of tired of talking for right now. Would you mind reading to me a bit? See there's a price to pay for my company," she said with a smile. "Sure, what do you want me to read?"

"There's a book over there Kay is reading to me. She has it marked where she left off."

Dax walked over and picked up the book that was open on the stand he had noticed earlier. He began reading without even looking to see what the name of the book was. From what he read, he gathered it was a book about the ladies of the Civil War. When he got to the bottom of the page he picked up the ribbon bookmark to lift it over to the next page. He froze when he saw the end of the bookmark was an upside-down cross. He thought, Should I just take it? She'll never know? Should I ask her about it. Maybe she knows more about what these crosses are for. He put the bookmark in the next page and started to read again, but his words were coming out slower. Ina noticed this right away, since her sense of hearing was very astute.

"Dax, what's the matter? You not feeling too perky yet after last night?"

"Well, Ina. No, it's not that. I have something to ask you, and I'm just not sure what your reaction will be."

"Well, you won't know till you ask, so just ask."

"Okay. The bookmark in this has an upside-down cross on it. Do you know where you got it?"

Ina sat up and turned her head in Dax's direction. "So you're finally here."

"What do you mean, I'm finally here?"

"My father gave me that cross in 1901, when I was nine years old. He told me someday someone would come looking for it and that I was never to let it out of my sight. I wore it for a lot of years under my clothes. No one ever came. I figured after fifty years, no one was coming, so I just kept it around."

"Do you know who gave it to your father?"

"I think he said it was some kind of scientist that was leaving the country, but that's about it."

"Ina, I was sent here to find this cross. There are others like it that, for some reason, are important to our government. I don't know any more than that. I have to ask you if I can have it."

"Sure, you can have it. I told my Father I would give it to the person that asked me for it, and that's you, so it's yours."

"Thank you."

"I suppose you'll be leaving now that you found what you've come for?"

"Yes, it seems pretty important that I get this back and find out what it means. Thank you, again. I won't forget you. I'm not too good about keeping in touch with people, but I will call you from time to time, if that's okay with you?"

"You bet. If I don't answer, call Kay. She'll come over and make sure I get the phone. And if you do find out what's so important about these crosses and if you can tell me, I'd sure like to know."

"Okay, I'll do that, even if I'm not supposed to. Bye."

"Bye, Dax. Nice talking to you."

# CHAPTER 10

Brand and Karen were on their way back home. They spent the rest of their time in Crested Butte hiking up to the top of the mountain, relaxing by the pool, and making love in the middle of the night. Brand needed the break, and Karen was happy. But now, they were on the road again, and Brand's mind was definitely back at work. He had gotten a call from Dax's old boss at Asphalt Specialties. Dax's friend Mike had passed away last night. The funeral would be Tuesday. Brand decided to wait until Dax got back to tell him. Dax had also called and told Brand the good news. He had the cross and would meet him at the office bright and early Monday morning.

When Dax got home, he had three messages from Peg. "Hey, where are you? I need to talk to you. Call me." Next message, "I guess you don't care what I have to say cause you didn't call back, but if you do care, call me." Third message, "Well, you must be gone—again. I should be used to this by now, but I'm not. Okay then. See you whenever. Bye." Dax called the 92nd Street bar, but Peg wasn't there. They wouldn't say where she was, and that was odd, because they all knew Peg and Dax were together. Something was different, but Dax didn't know what. He thought about going to the Bullet for a couple of drinks, but he really was tired and had had a few cocktails on the flight back.

Since tomorrow was Sunday, he knew Brand wouldn't call him until after church, so he called Scott, a friend from the bar and set up an early tee time for golf. He turned on the TV and lay on the floor. He was asleep within minutes. The Bullet opens at 7:00 AM every day except Wednesday, so Dax was there a few minutes before seven. JR was already there, along with Judy. Dax made Bloody Marys for the three of them. Everyone told him he made the best Bloody Marys .

The regular Sunday group who rode motorcycles together on the weekends in the summer started coming through the door.

"Hi, Judy, JR, Dax. How about three Bloody Marys and a diet Coke?" Judy took over and served up the drinks.

With his arm resting on his Striker golf clubs, Dax looked at one of the gals, Sandy, in the group and said, "You want to see my woody?" They all knew Dax and enjoyed his sense of humor. He never lacked for a comment or a comeback when the situation presented itself. The group drank up and headed out for their ride.

"You guys be careful," Dax said as they left.

Scott and Dax had just finished up and were putting their clubs in Scott's truck when Brand pulled up. "Thought I'd find you here. How'd you do?"

"Great, I beat Scott, and now he owes me a drink. Want to join us?"

"No thanks, I need to talk to you."

"Okay." Dax turned to Scott, "Go ahead, I'll catch up with you later."

"Alright, but your victory drink expires in two hours, cause I've got to go help Jimbo move some stuff at the house."

"Fair enough. See you later."

Brand opened the door for Dax. "Jump in. Where's the cross?" "Right here." Dax pulled up the chain from around his neck. " I didn't want to let it out of my sight." The cross was about two inches in length, yellow gold, with a silver X in the center where the two pieces met. It didn't look as elaborate as the others. In fact it was pretty simple in design.

"Let's take it to the office for safekeeping."

On the way to the office, Dax filled Brand in on the details of Ocean City and the people they met. Dax talked about Ina at length and told Brand that he would be keeping in touch with her. Brand looked at him sideways with a questioning expression.

"It's not what you think. She's a down-to-earth person who cares about people. That's all."

When they got to the office, Brand pulled out the case with the ten crosses and put this one in its place. Now there was only one missing.

"Do we know where we are suppose to find this last one?"

"Yes and no. Our sources say it is right here in Denver, but so far that is as close as they have come."

"Geez, it's not like that pinpoints it or anything. How do they even know it's here?"

"I wish I knew, but I'm not privy to that information. All I know is that they know it's here, and we need to find it soon. Grant and Carter are following up on the few leads we do have. Gage is still home recovering. He was hurt pretty bad."

"Yeah, that was a real bad deal."

"Dax, I want you to go down to the infirmary and get your contact replaced."

Dax looked at Brand with surprise. "Right now? How did you know I even lost it?"

"You told me you got smacked around in that fight, so I figured you must have gotten hit in the eye." Dax had his curiosity aroused now because he sure didn't remember telling Brand the details of the fight.

"Okay, I'll go do that now and see you in the morning."

"Before you go, there is something else I have to tell you. Sit down. Your old boss from Asphalt called. Mike died over the weekend. The funeral is Tuesday. I'm sorry."

Dax put is head down and was quiet for some time. When he looked up, his eyes were filling with tears. "Damn. Mike was a good person. He went out the way he wanted to—still working. I guess you know I'll be going to the funeral. Unless you need me here at the office early tomorrow, I think I'll go check on his family and hook up with you in the afternoon."

"That's fine. Since we haven't got a clue where in Denver this last cross is, we'll just keep in touch on the phone until Wednesday. Again, I'm sorry about Mike. I know he was a friend of yours."

"Thanks, see you later."

Dax was really down now and didn't want to talk to anyone, so he went to the infirmary, got his contact replaced, and headed for JR's. He had forgotten all about his wondering what was up with this contact thing. He meant to ask the doctor about it, but all he could think about was Mike.

At the Bullet, the regulars were holding down the fort. Larry, with his beer and water, Jimbo on his stool at the end of the bar, Gary shooting pool, Scott and Mark playing electronic golf and, Dick having his two beers before he headed home for the day. "Hey, there he is. I knew you'd show up to collect your drink!"

"Yeah, I'm here, but not to collect my free drink. I just found out one of my bridge crew died. He had cancer. He knew it and kept working up to the end. His family is sure gonna miss him."

JR sat down next to Dax. "Sorry to hear that. How long did he know he was dying?"

"About a year ago, they told him he had six months, so he made it past that, but you could tell he was really hurting these last couple of weeks."

Dax ended up staying at the bar later than usual. He was pretty drunk when he decided he needed to go home. Somehow he managed to make it home and passed out on the floor with his clothes on. He never shut his alarm off, so when it went off at 4:15 AM he woke up with a jump. He showered and shaved and threw a load of clothes in the laundry. He checked the frig for something cold to drink. V8 was looking pretty good, so he drank that down with a couple of aspirin and headed out the door.

On his way over to Mike's house, he was thinking about what he would say to Mike's wife, Helen. As he pulled up in front of the house, he took the cross Mike had given him and decided Mike's family might want to have it. Helen greeted Dax with a big hug and said how glad she was he came over. They talked for a while about Mike and about some of the times they spent together.

"Helen, Mike was one of the best people I knew. He never complained when things weren't going so good on the job. He was just glad to be there another day. This world could use more Mikes."

# CHAPTER 11

Grant and Carter were assigned to work up the leads ICO had on the last cross located somewhere in Denver. They decided to work together. They made a list of all the religious supply stores in the area. Grant said to Carter, "If anyone knows about any kind of cross that was made upside down, these people should."

"Okay, but let's go to the oldest one first. The older the better. These people usually know a lot about the history of religious stuff."

They used the good old yellow pages to start their search. To their surprise, they found only six in the heart of Denver, with a few others in the surrounding towns. Of the six, four were Catholic and two were Jewish. Since they were leaving from the Sugar building, located at the end of the 16th Street mall, they decided to go to the closest ones first.

The Gerken Church Supply store advertised itself as Colorado's largest. It was located in a poor, older section of town. The majority of the houses were flats with small stoops just a foot or two from the street. Several for sale signs were posted in the front of business windows long since shut down for lack of customers. This was definitely a neighborhood where people worked hard for their money and didn't have any left over for things they didn't need. When they entered the store, it was much larger on the inside than it appeared to be on the outside. Most of the items seemed to be of Catholic faith. Every wall was covered. There were medals, statues, pictures, holy water fountains, crucifixes, and more. What wasn't on the wall you could find in the rows of shelves—books, rosary beads, candles, nativity figures, Bibles, seraphim angels, and so on. There was also a side room strictly for clergy vestments.

As they perused the store, Carter asked the clerk to see several crosses in the window case. Though Carter was not brought up in the Catholic religion, he knew people who were serious about their religion believed theirs was the only true one. The cross that caught his eye was 24 kt. smooth gold with a silver rope chain that hung down from the middle. While it wasn't what he was looking for, he liked it because it was different. "How much is this one?"

"Let's see. It is $135.00 plus tax."

"Is that tax deductible?" he said with a smile.

"No 'fraid not, but it is very nice. Are you looking for something for yourself or for someone else?"

"Well, I wasn't really looking for anyone. This one just caught my eye. Have you ever seen a cross that was purposely made upside down?"

The clerk backed up a bit. "No, we would not sell one if we had one like that. They are disrespectful."

"Oh, I'm sorry. I didn't know that. I saw one on a pamphlet some guy handed me on the 16th Street mall and wondered why it was upside down, 'cause I'd never seen one like that either. If I remember right, this pamphlet was about 'Life after Death' and said that there was life after death for some, but not for others. It was kind of eerie."

Carter ended up buying a much more inexpensive cross for his son and thanked the clerk. When he turned around to look for Grant, he was gone. Now where did he disappear to? Carter hung around for a few more minutes, and when Grant didn't show, he left.

As Carter headed down the street, he saw an old brown van speed off around the corner. He was too late to get the license number. He had a bad feeling about this. "Hey, Brand, Carter here. Grant and I were just checking out the first place and I think something has happened to Grant. He's not in the store, and as I was leaving, an old beat-up brown van took off. I'm thinking maybe we should have someone in the air find and follow this van. Grant may be in it."

"Okay, I'll get someone up over there and hope we can find it. Why don't you come back here and tell me exactly what you did see over there?"

"Okay, will do. See you in a few."

By coincidence, Dax and Carter arrived at the front door of ICO at the same time. Carter was surprised to see Dax there. "Hey, what are you doing here? I thought you were going to take a couple of days off."

"Well, since I'm not doing much good anywhere else, I thought I'd see what you guys were up to," Dax explained.

"I think Grant was kidnapped from the religious supply store we were just at. One minute he was there, and the next he was gone. Brand sent a 'copter out to look for the van I think he was taken in," Carter said.

"When did this happen?" Dax asked.

"Just about fifteen minutes ago." Carter answered.

"What did the van look like?"

"It was an old junker, brown, paint gone here and there, and dents all over it, like hail damage." Carter told him.

"Christ, I just passed a wreck on I-25 at 20th Street. It looked like a semi-trailer full of cars turned over on top of a van like that. We'd better get over there."

"Shouldn't we call Brand first?"

"We'll call him on the way. Let's go!"

It only took Dax and Carter five minutes to reach the on ramp to I-25, but traffic was already backed up for miles in both directions on the highway. No cars were being allowed near the wreck. All Dax and Carter could do was watch as the fire trucks and ambulances arrived. It looked like the van underneath was flattened. No one could have survived the wreck.

"Brand, Dax here. Carter is here with me. We think we found the van Grant was in. It was just crushed by a semi on I-25 and we can't get anywhere near it. Maybe you should contact the Denver police and find out where they are taking the victims. We can back track out of this jam and head straight there."

"Okay, I'll call you back. Sit tight."

Brand called his friend, Lieutenant Brown, at the Sheriff's department and asked if he could find out where the victims were being taken. "Hold on." Brand could see the accident scene on the TV. The noon news was flashing the highway back up alert across the bottom on the screen. "Brand, they are taking one person to St. Anthony's North and two to the city morgue."

"Oh, God. Do you know the names yet?"

"Sorry, no, but I'll call you as soon as I have them."

"Okay, thanks."

As Dax and Carter backtracked so they could get back onto the highway, Carter's cell phone rang. "Carter, head over to the morgue first, since that is closer."

"Okay. God, I hope Grant's not there."

"Me too."

The paramedics were wheeling the bodies in the back door just as Dax and Carter pulled into the parking lot in front. When they got to the front desk, they explained why they were there. They were asked to take a seat in the waiting room and someone would be with them. They waited for forty-five minutes before Dax went to the front desk again. "How long do we have to wait?"

"It shouldn't be much longer."

"Can you at least call down and find out when we can I.D. the bodies?" Dax was a little more on edge than usual, with Mike's funeral tomorrow, this case being so critical, and not hearing anything from Peg for over a week now. He wasn't going to take any crap from anyone.

51

"Okay, just please have a seat."

Ten minutes later, the medical examiner sat down next to Carter.

"Who are you here to identify."

"Our partner, Grant Sherman."

"Are you a relative?"

"No, I just told you we worked with him."

"Can you give me a description first, so I know which person to show you?"

"Oh for crying out loud," Dax said as he stood up. "Didn't you find his driver's license?"

"Calm down, please. There was no I.D. of any kind on one of them. The only thing we have is a cross we found in his shoe."

"A cross? Did this cross happen to be different than most crosses?"

"I don't think so, it looked like a regular cross to me."

"Can we see it?"

"Stay here. I'll get it."

When the M.E. returned, he held the cross out flat in his hand. It looked normal to the M.E., but that was because he had it upside down in his hand, which meant it was one of the crosses they had been looking for. Dax excused himself and went outside. "Brand, one of the crosses we are looking for was on one of the bodies. The M.E. won't let us I.D. the body because we aren't relatives. What should we do?"

"Just come back to ICO, I'll take care of it."

"Okay."

Dax went back inside. "Thanks, we'll be going now. Come on, Carter. Brand wants us back to work." They got in the car.

"Now what? We have to get that cross."

"Brand said he would take care of it. I'm more concerned as to who the cross was on? If Grant is in there, I sure hope this case is worth his life."

Dax dropped Carter off at the Sugar building.

"Aren't you coming in?"

"No, I'll check in later. This thing with Mike and now maybe Grant is getting scary. I think I'll go chill for a while."

# CHAPTER 12

"Shot of peppermint and a rum and Coke," Dax said as he sat down on the bar stool.

"You look like you've just lost your last friend," Judy said.

"I might have." Judy had just started working at JR's last week. She had never been a bartender before, but it seemed to come easy to her. She waited on everyone as if they were her only customer. "So, did you really lose a friend?"

"Yeah, one of my best crew guys died."

"Sorry."

"Thanks." Dax didn't say much for the next hour. He just watched Jerry Springer with the rest of the usuals and drank until he was tired.

Brand called bright and early the next day. "Dax I need you to come to the office now."

"Any word on Grant?"

"Yeah. Sorry to say, he was killed in the accident. I know this is bad for you, but we need to move really fast now. The last cross we needed was the one on Grant."

"Okay, I'll be there in half an hour."

When Dax arrived, Gage and Carter were also there. They took a moment to think about Grant. They were going to miss him on their team. Brand had the crosses all in the case in front of him. "Gage and Carter, I can't thank you enough for sticking your necks out on this one. You two will get another assignment, and Dax here is going on a little vacation."

"Hey, how come he gets the vacation? Is he special or somethin'?" Gage protested.

"Now you know better than that. You two are needed elsewhere right now, and he isn't, that's all." They shared handshakes and pats on the back all around.

After Gage and Carter left the room, Brand turned to Dax. "Well, would you like to know where you are going on vacation?"

"Oh great. If you already know where it is, then it must not really be a vacation."

"Have you ever been to the Pentagon?"

"No, and there isn't anything I want to see there either."

"That's what you think. Do you know what is even better than going to D.C.?"

"No, but I'm sure you are going to tell me." Dax sighed.

"I am going with you!" Brand could not contain his smile when he saw Dax's expression.

Brand and Dax arrived in D.C. midday the following day. They checked into an older hotel two blocks from the White House. While they were checking in, Brand told Dax they were expected at the Pentagon at 7:00 PM that night. "Why so late?"

"Because almost everyone will be gone by then, and that's when the Secretary of State is available."

"What? Hey, you know I'm not into this big time stuff. Why don't you just go and tell me what happens?"

"Because they want someone just like you to keep them from going off in the wrong direction, and because I picked you for this assignment."

"Oh, guess I should take that as compliment, thanks."

Brand knew that would get him. "I would suggest that you get a nap this afternoon because I don't think this is going to be a short night. I'll meet you back here at 6:00 PM."

Dax put his clothes in the room and flopped back on the bed. He closed his eyes for about three minutes. He glanced at the phone. The red message light was blinking. Must be Brand, he thought. He dialed the numbers to retrieve the message. "If you know what is good for you, you will not go to the meeting tonight. You are in danger and so is your boss." The caller hung up.

Now Dax was irritated. Who in the heck even knew he was here? And how could they even leave a message before he checked in? He thought about this for a minute. It had to be someone with ICO. They always knew where he was. But why would someone from inside leave a message for him and not Brand? Or maybe they did. He would check with Brand on the way to their meeting later.

He decided to go for a walk. He started to walk towards the White House. The usual line of tourists was there. He noticed the military inside the grounds actually had weapons, and it looked like they took their job seriously. He headed away from the White House. He saw a place called Old Ebbet's Bar and Dining. Well, he thought, one drink wouldn't hurt, and he was a little hungry. Unbeknownst to Dax, this establishment was well known in D.C. A lot of Congressmen and lobbyists hung out here. The fine wood floors and brass railings shone. This was definitely old money.

He always preferred eating at the bar, so he found one in the back and settled in. The bartender looked like he was dressed for a wedding. "What's your specialty?" Dax asked him.

"The best margarita you will ever have in your whole life is just minutes away."

Dax grinned, "I'm not really a margarita man, but I'm always willing to try anything once. Set me up."

The bartender performed his best as the margarita was being prepared. "Would you like to see a menu?"

"Sure. I don't suppose you could recommend something?"

This was going to be a good tip, the bartender thought. "Well, sure. We have the best hamburgers on the hill."

"Okay, well since this will be my first one on the hill, I might as well have the best."

Dax had to agree, the drink was very good—potent, but not sour. The hamburger vanished in a few bites, so he put down a twenty-dollar tip, raised his hand at the bartender, and said, "Thanks."

"Say, be careful walking around down here after dark, your first time and all. You can't tell who the crooks are in this town by the way they dress!"

Dax chuckled and made his way back to the hotel.

Brand was in the lobby waiting when Dax walked in. "I see you took my advice and got some sleep," he said sarcastically.

"Well, you know me. I get restless." As they got into the cab, Dax asked Brand. "Say, did you have a message on your phone?"

"No, did you call me?"

"No, but I had a message from someone who didn't leave their name."

"What did they say?"

"Something like, 'Don't go this meeting' that we are about to go to and that we are both in trouble."

Brand's forehead wrinkled a bit. "Well, who do you think it was?"

"Darned if I know. I thought you would know."

"No, I don't have a clue, but it doesn't change anything." Dax turned and looked out the window, it had started to rain. In the back of his mind he had the feeling Brand wasn't being up-front with him. He had never doubted Brand before, so he wasn't sure why he doubted him now.

# CHAPTER 13

The Secretary of State met Brand and Dax personally at the door. Dax was a little intimidated to say the least. "I see you have it," the Secretary said as he looked at Brand's briefcase.

"It hasn't been out of my sight."

"Good." There was no more conversation.

They were lead through several corridors. They walked up a flight of stairs, and then took an elevator that looked like a closet when you walked into it. They were going up, but there were no numbers anywhere to indicate what floor they were going to. They finally entered a large room, vinyl floor, no windows and very dim lighting.

The Secretary faced the two of them and said, "The White House and the country is counting on the two of you. Here is a phone you can use if you need anything. It rings directly to me, no one else. Call me if you need anything or when you have something to tell me. We have rooms set up for you in the back. If you need to make a personal call, call me, and I will put your call through. Good luck, and let me know when you have something, anything."

As the Secretary shut the door, Dax said, "Just what are we supposed to find, and how are we supposed to find it if we are shut up in this room?" Once more, Brand took the role of mentoring Dax. At the end of the room was a row of computers, twelve in all. Brand walked over to them and sat down at the first one. "We are going to find whatever it is in these." Dax was slightly upset now because he really did not know much about computers and didn't want Brand to think he was stupid. But he sat down at the computer next to Brand and just did what Brand did. Brand pushed the 'on' button and waited. Dax did the same. The screen came up on both of them, but there was nothing on them.

"These things must be broken. There isn't anything on the screen," Dax said. Both of them spent the next couple of minutes tapping on different combinations of keys and buttons. Then, all of a sudden, Dax's CD drive opened. "What the heck?" Brand looked over at the disc drive on Dax's machine. The shape of the drive was in the shape of a cross! Dax looked at Brand. "You thinkin' what I'm thinkin'"?

"Yep." Brand unlocked the briefcase and looked over the crosses. He picked up the one that looked like it matched the shape of the CD drive.

Dax set it inside the drive and pushed it slightly. When the drive closed the computer made whirring sounds. The screen went blank for a few seconds. The next thing they saw was the Presidential seal as big as the screen with the letters D.O.D across it. The two of them sat silent for a few seconds. Dax finally broke the silence by saying "What the heck does the Department of Defense have to do with these crosses we have? This is not making any sense to me! Is there anything you would like to tell me now that we have gotten this far?"

Brand said, "I really don't know much more than you at this point, other than we have to find some information in these computers that is top secret, and our government needs to know it before anyone else does. I don't know if whatever this is will be a good thing or a bad thing. I only know that when we find it, we will know we have found it."

They spent the next few minutes putting the rest of the crosses in the CD drives of the other computers. They got a surprise when they put the last one in. When the last one closed, the Presidential seal on all the computers went away and a folder was displayed on each desktop. Each computer had a folder with a title of the months of the year. Going down the row, January on the first one, February on the second, continuing down to December on the last one.

Brand said, "Well, let's see what we have." He double clicked on the January folder. When he opened it, there was a menu that had the fifty-two states of the United States listed. He double clicked on Alabama. The next menu had what looked like a list of hospitals on it.

After watching Brand, Dax sat down at the next computer and opened the folder for Alaska. When the list of hospitals came up, he clicked on the first one. What he saw next was a menu of just the alphabet. He opened the A folder. For the next 20 seconds all he saw was a blur of pages speed up on the screen. He couldn't make out what the pages were until it finally stopped.

"This is weird. Brand, look at this."

Brand leaned over to take a look. "I know, I have the same thing. We are looking at birth certificates."

"This is getting stranger and stranger."

For the next several hours, they opened folder after folder on every computer. Their eyes were strained and tired. Each computer had every state and every letter of the alphabet for the lists of hospitals. They all had thousands and thousands of birth certificates in their files. The only difference in the computers was that each one only had one month.

They called for some coffee and snacks. This was going to be a long night. They looked at hundreds of birth certificates. Some had pictures of the hospitals. Some had baby footprints on them. Some were in color, others in black and white. They worked individually for hours, not knowing what they would find. They were trying to make connections on what they were seeing. They made a list.

Same child's first names.

Same hospital names in different states.

Same last names born same year.

Same doctor names in different hospitals.

Same date of each month for each year.

Same days of the week for each month for each year for same names, etc. etc. etc. The list of common possibilities seemed to go on forever. They ended up with over sixty possible "like" combinations.

When they completed listing over half of the possible links, they were beat. They decided to rest, it was already noon. Brand was sleeping hard within minutes. After listening to Brand's heavy breathing for a few minutes, Dax drifted off.

"Sir, sir, wake up please. Sir, I need you to come with me now."

Dax looked at the Marine through sleepy eyes and said, "What? Who are you? Where am I?"

The Marine stood tall in his dress whites, and did not crack a smile. "There is a phone call for you. You can take it right outside the door."

"Okay, but who would be calling me here?"

"Even if I knew, sir, I would not be at liberty to say."

"Oh brother," Dax said under his breath.

"Hello."

"Hi, Dad! I need some help."

"Dade, I just sent you some money last week. What now?"

"No, it's not that. My science teacher wants me to write a paper about something called DNA, just because I told some kid he was a jerk. The kid didn't even know the difference between an X or Y chromosome!"

Dax had to chuckle to himself. Leave it to kids to bring you back to reality. "Dade, not everyone is interested in science like you. You should have just explained it to him."

"Oh yeah, I did that alright. The teacher made me get up in front of the class and explain it to everyone! And then the teacher said I did such a good job of that, I have to write this dumb paper now. It isn't fair."

"So what do you want me to do, write the paper for you?"

"No, but since we don't have a computer, I can't get online to find stuff about it. I thought maybe you could do it with your work computer and send me the stuff."

Dax thought for a minute. "When do you have to have the report done?"

"Two weeks."

"Okay, I'll see what I can do, but I probably can't get you anything for a couple of days, okay?"

"Cool! That will be great, Dad. Thanks. I miss you. Love you, got to go now."

"I love you too, now be a little nicer to your school friends, or no more favors, got it?

"Got it. Bye."

The Marine stood next to Dax the whole time he was on the phone. When Dax hung up he said, "Is there anything you need, sir?"

"As a matter of fact, there is. I need some information about DNA for a report my son has to do for school. Can you get me something I can send to him?"

"I'll check with the Secretary and let you know. Anything else?"

"Now that you ask, how about a rum and Coke?"

"Sorry, sir. No alcohol is allowed on the premises. Would you like a soft drink or coffee?"

"Coffee it is, then. Thanks."

Dax went back in the room and lay down on the bed. Brand was still sleeping soundly. Dax dozed off until his pager vibration woke him up. He read the screen, "If you haven't found it by now, you had better hurry! You are wasting precious time." Again there was no signature or clue as to who was sending him these messages.

The Marine was back. "Say, how did my son know where to call me? I didn't think anyone knew where I was?"

"We simply forwarded your calls here, so he thinks he reached you at home."

"Are you listening to my phone calls?"

"Here is your coffee and articles on DNA." With that, he turned and left, locking the door on his way out.

# CHAPTER 14

It had been awhile since Dax read anything other than the daily paper. He wasn't sure how much of this DNA information he could read without getting bored. Coincidentally, one of the first articles in the stack was from the Denver Post. It talked about genetic fingerprinting. It said the human body is built from about sixty trillion cells, and DNA's genetic blueprint is stored on twenty-three pairs of chromosomes in the nucleus of each cell. The Fort Collins Research Center had been doing work profiling and looking for patterns of diseases within the DNA. For example, the bacteria that causes plague is a single-celled organism with one lone chromosome in the nucleus of each cell. The researchers used a special dye to light up DNA, then a photo was taken of the distinctive pattern. These were categorized according to what type of disease was found. Okay, that was interesting, Dax thought, but kids are probably not interested in the plague.

The next article, from a medical insurance company's health journal, talked about decoding a person's genetic makeup. It stated that it took ten years to identify the 30,000 genes contained in every human cell and determine the sequence of about three billion pairs of bases that make up DNA. "Boy! Is that job security or what?" Dax said to himself. The article went on to say the medical advantage for the insurance companies was that this sequencing could be used to improve diagnostic testing. Doctors could do genetic tests for MS, cystic fibrosis, and other rare conditions. Common diseases were harder to test for since their patterns were not as a unique as the more uncommon diseases. That, plus diseases usually stem from several genes, plus the environment, and lifestyle choices. Dax read a few more paragraphs and decided this information would not cut it for 8th graders either.

DNA: A waiting game was the title of the next document. The Colorado Bureau of Investigation has a backlog of three and one-half months of criminal cases waiting for DNA analysis. Last year alone they received 600 cases with more than 3,200 pieces of evidence. Dax had seen the TV shows about forensic science finding people guilty of crimes with just a drop of human spit! DNA was also used to reopen cases of convicted criminals who were then proven innocent. He didn't quite understand how all that worked, but he found it pretty interesting.

Dax decided his son would probably find this stuff pretty neat, so he called the Marine and asked him if he could mail these articles to his son.

"Sure, anything else?"

"Now that you mention it, can you guys tell where a message is coming from on a pager?"

"I don't know, sir, but I will find out. Do you have a pager with you that you want us to look at?"

"Yep, here it is, but I would like to have it back right away, if I can." The Marine took the pager without an answer and locked the door behind him—again. Dax said under his breath, Geez, like I'm gonna try to escape from the Pentagon. I couldn't find my way out of this maze if I wanted to."

Dax decided to go back to the computers. He started looking at the birth certificates again. He printed out several different types and studied them. He and Brand had had no luck with all their ideas about a common thread using all the information on the certificates, so he just laid them out on a table. There was about twenty of them, all colors, all sizes, and no two were alike.

The printers woke Brand up, so he walked over to Dax. "Well, have you cracked the case?"

"What do you think?"

"I think you're standing here and haven't got a clue."

"Pretty much, but, let me run this by you. What if what we are looking for is not so complicated, but is really something so simple we are overlooking it?"

"For example?" Brand thought he would indulge his buddy.

"Well, just look at these and tell me what you see that is common about the document, but not about what they say on them."

"You mean like, they are all from hospitals, they all have places for name, date of birth, parents name, and doctor's name."

"Yep, like that. Now come over here to the computer and look at the same document on the screen. Do you see anything different from the printed copy to what is on the screen?"

Brand studied each screen with the copy in his hand. After thirty minutes, he said, "I give up, I don't see anything different. Do you?"

"Well, I'm not sure. It could be my bad eye acting up again. That's why I wanted you to look at these to see if you noticed what I did."

"Well, I don't, so why don't you tell me what you see?"

Just then the Marine came in the room. "Sir, you have another page we thought you would want to see."

"Another page?" Brand asked. "You've been getting pages here and not telling me?"

"I planned on telling you as soon as I found out who was sending them." Dax turned to the guard before he read the page. "Did you find out where they are coming from?"

"All we know for now is that they are coming from the Denver area. If you give us more time, we might be able to give you an address or something."

"Denver? Can I see the page now?" It read, "YOU ARE GETTING VERY CLOSE, KEEP GOING."

Brand was not happy. "Do you want to tell me what is going on?"

"If I knew, I would tell you. I have been getting pages since we got to Washington. Stuff like I had better hurry up and figure this out before it is too late, and now this one."

"Well, that's just dandy! Close to what? We don't even know what the heck we are looking for!"

Dax handed the pager back to the Marine and said, "Thanks."

Dax turned to Brand. "Okay, calm down. Let's go back to what we were doing. What is bothering me is, How can someone in Denver see what I'm doing to know that I—I mean we are getting close?"

Brand's face turned a little red.

Dax saw his expression, "So you have something to tell me. You wouldn't be keeping me in the dark about anything now, would you?"

"Time to come clean, I guess, but remember, you signed on for this work, so don't pitch a fit when I tell you. That, ah, 'bad eye' you have that we keep putting a new contact on ? Well, the contact is really a remote camera that sends what you are seeing, saying, and hearing  back to headquarters. That's how we know where you are going and what you are doing. It is really for your own protection." Brand stopped talking at that point to see what Dax was going to say or do. Dax didn't say anything for a good minute.

"All right. Anything else I should know?"

"Nope, that's pretty much it, unless of course you are wondering if everyone has one of these special eyes. The answer is no. You are our test case. So far, the only time we lost contact with you was when you got in that fight in Ocean City. Not much we could do about that. You okay?"

"Yeah, so do you plan on keeping it in there?"

"As long as you are working for us we do. But now I think we have a problem, because apparently someone else is watching you besides us. From what that last page said, I think we may have put you in more danger than we know. So let's get back to business so we can get home and change out that contact."

"Why don't I just take it out now?"

"Hold on. Let me check with headquarters first."

Brand asked for an outside line to make his call. He was taken to another room so Dax would not be able to hear what he was saying. While Brand was gone, Dax pulled up his and Brand's birth certificates. Who better to know if what was on these had something on them that wasn't right than them? Dax's birthday was September 1, 1958. Brand's birthday was December 24, 1954. Dax printed them out and compared them to the screen. He was sitting there staring at the two certificates when Brand came back in the room. "Sorry, headquarters says they want you to keep it on, especially since someone else is watching. The government guys are working on locating the source of the pages."

Brand looked at the computers and saw his and Dax's certificates. "What are you doing?"

"Well, look at yours. See anything wrong?"

Brand read the information and said, "No, looks right to me."

"Mine too, but we are missing something. It must be so simple we can't see it."

"Sir, sorry to bother you." The Marine was back again. "Your daughter is on the phone now. You can pick it up over there on the white phone."

"Hi, Solei, honey, what's up?"

"Who was that that answered your phone?"

"Oh, just a friend of mine." Solei didn't like anyone getting between her and her dad.

"You just let anyone answer your phone? Why didn't you answer?"

Dax rolled his eyes, "Solei, honey, I was in the bathroom. Now what do you want, honey?"

"Oh, I need a copy of my birth certificate for school so I can go on a field trip to Washington D.C. Mom says you have the original, and she doesn't have time to go get me another copy."

Man oh man, Dax thought, Solei could still make him mad by pulling these stunts. "Okay, honey. I'll send it registered mail. Mom will have to sign for it when it comes so I know you got it. It should be there in a couple of days. Call me when you get it, okay?"

"Okay, Dad. I knew I could count on you! But I still don't think you should let just anyone answer your phone! Love you, bye!"

With a smile, Dax said, "Love you too, be good. Say, when is your trip?" But the next thing he heard was the dial tone, she had already hung up.

Dax hung up the phone and turned around. Mr. Marine was still standing at attention. He said to Dax, "I'll take care of it, sir. Do you want to write a note to put with it?"

"Yeah, that would be a good idea." Dax wasn't much of a writer of anything, but he knew Solei would get a kick out of getting a note from him. Roses are red, Violets are blue, Sugar is sweet and so am I (and you!) Love, Your Favorite Dad.

He knew it wasn't too original, but that was okay. His daughter would love it.

# CHAPTER 15

For the rest of the day and well into the night, Brand and Dax kept at it. By noon the next day, they weren't any closer to finding anything that would be a clue as to what information was in the birth certificates that the Department of Defense would be interested in. They needed a break, so they asked to see the Secretary of Defense. They had to wait until late afternoon before he arrived. "You have something for me?"

Brand answered for them both. "No, sir, we are stuck. We need to take our minds off this for a bit so we can come back with a fresh approach."

"Okay. How about you go back to Denver for a couple of days, and then come back and see what you can do?"

"Can we afford the two days?"

"Well, if you aren't getting anywhere, you are not doing much good here. How about this, if you think of something, anything, get back here ASAP, okay?"

"Okay."

Dax was so glad to be going home. He relaxed on the plane, had a few cocktails, and headed straight for JR's.

"Dax, I'll be calling you day after tomorrow, so don't get into any trouble between now and then."

"You know me, Brand. I go out of my way to stay out of trouble."

"Yeah, right."

The regulars at JR's greeted Dax with some hearty back slaps and jokes about where the heck he had been. Dax was always good to come back with something. "Well, I've been to Florida. My boss is thinking about sending me down there for work, so I thought I would check it out."

Just then JR walked in. "Hey. Did you miss me?"

"Well, sure. We've been lacking for entertainment around here. Let me buy you a shot."

"Alrighty then. It is good to be home."

When Dax finally got home, he had a stack of mail, mostly bills, but he saw a handwritten letter from Paula. He threw it all on the floor and then threw himself on the floor and slept all night. When his alarm went off at 5:00 AM he woke up cursing to himself. "Damn it, who set that alarm?" Of course Dax had never unset the alarm before he left, so he knew it was his own doing.

After a shower and shave, he headed for the Daylight Donut shop at 120th and Colorado, conveniently located in the same strip mall as JR's.

He ordered the breakfast burrito, coffee, and milk. While he was waiting for his food, he started going through his mail. There was mostly bills and junk, so he skipped through those pretty fast. When he got to the letter from Paula, he hesitated. He knew this could not be good news. It was only one short page, so he knew the pain would be swift.

Dear Dax,

Where are you? Not here, and here is where I need you to be. I have come to care a lot for you, and that was my mistake. We had some great times, but now I have to say good-bye. I have to make a better life for myself and my kids. They come first.

I have come to learn that no matter what I say or what I do, I will never be the last person you say good-night to and the first person you say good morning to every day—and that is what I need and want.

You know I want the best for you. Take care.

Love, Paula.

Well, there is was in writing. He couldn't blame her. He knew he wasn't the most stable person or the best role model for kids, so that was that. The next thing to do, of course, was to eat his breakfast, Western Union some money for the kids, and go to JR's.

He sat there in his sweat pants and T-shirt reading the paper. Sherri was behind the bar stocking the coolers. "You okay?" she asked, not looking up at Dax.

"Yep. You need help back there?"

"Well, since you're askin', could you count the cans in the trash? I didn't get that done yet."

"Sure." Dax knew his way around the bar, both in front and behind. He helped out whenever he was asked or when he was in the mood. A few people started trickling in. Larry, Dick, Gary—they sat around the island so they could talk with each other and Dax. "So what's been happening since I've been gone?"

Larry spoke first. "Well, me and the Mrs. moved down south, so it takes me a little longer to get home, that's all." Larry pointed over to Gary and said, "Deb and Gary went and got married, moved to a new house, and are still speaking to each other."

"No kiddin'—that's major. What brought that on? You guys been goin' together for twelve years, why get married now?"

Gary shrugged his shoulder, "Thought I would make a respectable man out of myself. I ain't gettin' younger. And besides, who else would put up with me?"

"You got a point there," Dax said as he thought about what Paula said in her letter.

"So, Dick, you married Rita yet?"

"No, not yet—we're still trying to figure out if we like each other!"

"Nothing wrong with that." Dax went back to reading the paper. He usually read the national stuff, sports, and sometimes the business section. When he closed the paper, the obituary notices were on the back. He started to read the names just to see how old these folks were. It always made him wince when he saw a young age on an obit. Tom Dittmer, 55, Thornton, CO. Date of Death, August 7, 2001. Originally from Davenport, Iowa. Worked for twenty-five years as an electrician. Survived by his wife, Sharon, and daughter, Lindsey. Donations may be made to your favorite charity.

"Hey, is this the Tom guy that comes in here every Friday, gets plastered, and then we don't see him for another week?"

"Yep, that's him. He ran off the road at Hwy 7 and I-25. Hit a concrete wall."

"Damn. That is too bad." Dax put the paper down. It was noon now, so he thought he should have a drink. "Rum and Coke, Sherry."

Brand could not wait to get home to Karen. They made love as soon as they were alone and slept all night in each other's arms. As Karen was making breakfast, she asked, "So did you finish what you needed to do in D.C.?"

"No, I'm really frustrated that we didn't. I don't want to talk about it. The purpose of me coming home was to take my mind off it. I'm hoping something will just pop into my head and Voila! I'll have the answer."

"Okay, how about we take a ride in the mountains, breathe some great fresh air, and go to the Red Lion for dinner?"

"That sounds like a great plan to me. I'll go clean up the bike." He gave Karen a kiss on the forehead on the way to the garage. He took the cover off the Road King and smiled. He loved his bike and thought Karen was pretty smart to know this was just the thing to take his mind off work. After a quickie water and rag wash, he put the jackets, camera, and binoculars in the bags. He popped his head in the door, "You ready?"

"I'll be ready in 5 minutes."

Brand pulled out a lawn chair and sat in the driveway waiting. It was a great day. The sun was out. The temperature was 60 already, and he was going for a ride! "Hi, Brand," his across-the-street neighbor said as he waved.

"Hi, Steve. You guys headed over to Melanie's?" Melanie was Steve and Bonnie's daughter. She had two children, Elise and Josh. Steve was loading them into the car.

"Hi, Brand," Josh yelled. He always said hi to Brand. Brand was his buddy.

"Hi, Josh. Did you have fun spending the night at Grandma and Grandpa's?"

"Yep!"

"Okay. See you later, Josh. See you, Steve."

Karen was ready to go. They climbed on the bike and headed for Estes Park. There were a couple of ways to get to Estes Park. Brand decided to go up I-25 to Longmont, through Lyons and up the Canyon. In Lyons they stopped at a new bar called The Outlaw. It had just opened a month ago. There were several bikes parked outside. Everything inside had been gutted, and it was now a clean, mountain resort type place. Because of the name alone, it attracted bikers. There were tables outside and a huge grill. On the walls were several biker flyer events. Red Hill, a bike shop two blocks away, was having a hog roast next week end. Brand showed Karen the flyer. "I'd like to go to this next weekend. Do we have anything planned?"

"No, not that I know of."

"Hey, Brand. Good to see you."

Brand turned around, "Well, Kelly! How are you? We sure do run into you everywhere."

"Hi, Karen. When it is this nice out, I don't stay home."

"What have you been up to?"

"Well, I have some good news and some bad news," Kelly said with a serious face. He hardly ever smiled, so people thought he was mean, but he really was a nice guy.

"What happened?"

"Well, I was at the Trailside Saloon last month on a weeknight. I went out a couple of times to check on my bike cause there aren't any windows there, you know. Then I went out to leave, and my bike was stolen!"

"Oh no! You're kidding me?"

"No, it was gone."

"Oh man, that is awful! I don't suppose they found it?"

"No. It is long gone. But about two weeks after that happened, I was at a place, and this girl was selling raffle tickets to win a bike. I was trying to get the girl to go out with me, so I bought some tickets. A week later, I get this call that says I won the bike."

"Oh man, I don't believe it," Brand said all smiles. "That is great!"

"Yep, so I got the bike, traded it in, and got me a new bike, plus I still get insurance money back from the one that got stolen."

"I can't believe it. That is quite a story. Good for you!"

"Yeah, it all worked out. But I never did get a date with the girl."

Brand and Karen laughed. "Well, you can't win them all. Hey good see-ing you. We're going to head on up the mountain. Catch you later."

"Okay, see you around."

# CHAPTER 16

After a great day of riding and a fabulous dinner, Brand and Karen got home about 8:00 PM. There was some daylight left, so they sat on the back deck and enjoyed the backyard. The phone broke the silence they were enjoying. "Do you want me to get it?"

"Sure, it's probably for one of the kids anyway."

Karen came back with the phone in her hand. "I think it is somebody you work with, but I can't understand a word he is saying. I think he is drunk."

Brand took the phone. "That can only be Dax."

"Dax, what's up?"

"Brnd I thnk I knw wz we r msng."

"What?"

"I thnk I knw wz we r msng."

"Okay." Brand gave Karen a wink. "Can you drive home okay, or do I need to come get you?"

"I got a ride."

"Okay, you go home, and I will call you. Go home now. Okay?"

"K. Latr."

At 5:45 AM Brand called Dax. He knew his alarm would be set for 5:30 AM, so he wanted to give him a minute to wake up. "Good morning. How you feeling this morning?"

"Wise guy you are."

"Do you remember calling me last night?"

"Of course I do."

"Do you remember what you said? I sure hope so, cause I couldn't understand one word of it."

Dax laughed. "Yeah I remember, but I'm not going to tell you now. We need to get back to D.C. Then I'll tell you."

"Really? You sure you don't want to give me a clue in case we are making this trip for nothing?"

"No, we need to go. I'll meet you at the airport in a couple of hours. You can get us flights, right?"

"Yep, see you at 9:00 AM West terminal, baggage claim."

"Okay, bye."

Brand told Karen he had to go back to work. She was really disappointed but knew this was the way it was.

"I think we may be wrapping this one up."

"Love you. Hurry back."

"Love you too."

"Well? You gonna share your brainstorm with me, or do I have to be kept in suspense until you're ready?"

Dax knew Brand did not like to be kept waiting, but until he checked his theory out, there was no point in getting his hopes up and besides, if Dax was right, there was a couple of things he wanted to do before spilling the beans. "Well, if you won't get too mad, I'd really like to wait until I check it out with the computers. Believe me, if I am right, it is not good, for anyone."

Dax added, "And just so you know, I have not talked to anyone or written anything down so the guys back at headquarters don't even know what I am thinking, now that I know how they are keeping my eye on myself."

Brand smiled, "I knew that would tick you off, once you found out, but you handled it pretty well. Okay, let's have a drink and enjoy the ride."

It was early evening by the time they got to the Pentagon. Brand had called ahead to let the Marines in charge know they would be arriving. "Welcome back. Is there anything I can get you?" It was the same Marine that had stood watch over them last time.

"Don't you ever get a day off?" Dax asked.

"Not until this assignment is over, sir."

"Okay then, how about some strong coffee and a steak medium rare."

"And for you, sir," the Marine asked, turning to Brand.

"I'll have the same, thanks."

"Oh! And one more thing, could you bring me today's newspaper?"

"Which one, sir?"

"It doesn't matter, any paper." The door was locked behind them. Brand sat at the computer next to Dax. "You dragged us all the way back here to read the paper?"

"No, just wait." Dax pulled out the Rocky Mountain News from two days ago.

"What? You gonna just read the paper now?" Brand was starting to get irritated.

71

"How about you go over there and wait for our dinner. You can watch me from there."

"Fine, I'll be right here, watching you."

Dax turned the paper to the obit on Tom Dittmer. It said he was from Davenport, Iowa, age 52. So that meant he was born in 1949. Dax pulled up the hospital names in Davenport in 1949. Two showed up. Mercy Hospital and St. Lukes Hospital. That was good, only two. He checked St. Lukes first for all babies born that year with the last name of Dittmer. There were over 100, but only seven with Tom as the first name. He pulled those records aside and then checked Mercy hospital. This time he got a match on ten Toms.

He put all the Tom Dittmer birth records into one file. When he had them all together, he took them one by one, blew them up on the screen and gave each one a really hard look. Now he knew headquarters was watching, so he would have to be very careful if he found something out of the ordinary. He'd gone through about half of them, when he thought he saw something unusual in the notary public seal on the certificate. He couldn't be sure, so he printed that certificate out.

When he got up to get the print, the door opened. The well built Marine had their steaks and newspaper. "How did you get this cushy job anyway?" Dax asked him.

"Is there anything else I can get you, sir?"

"No, not for me."

"Me either," Brand added. Brand was still irritated with Dax. "That cushy job Marine could clean your clock without breaking a sweat."

"Don't I know it. I was just trying to get him to open up a little, but I can see he takes his job very seriously."

"Okay then, let's eat!"

"What did you print off over there."

"Just one of the birth certificates. I want to take a really good look at it."

"We've already done that, haven't we?"

"Yes, but now I have something that I think looks different." They finished their dinner with few words spoken. Afterwards, Brand checked in with the office, while Dax went back to work.

"So what's he lookin at?" Brand asked?"

The "eyes" in Denver replied, "He's looking at a birth certificate for a guy by the name of Tom Dittmer who was killed in a car wreck a couple of days ago. He found seventeen of them for the same name in the year this guy was born."

"Okay, but why did he print only this one?"

"Don't know that yet, but I'll page you when we figure it out."

"Okay, good."

Dax kept looking back and forth from the printed birth certificate to the certificate on the screen. There was definitely something different in the seal on the one in the computer. He kept his eyes moving so that headquarters would not know just what he was looking at. He just couldn't be sure what his eyes saw, so he decided to play around with the colors on the screen. He changed the background colors and the lettering colors several times. He tried blue with red, black with orange, white with purple. There were about sixty-four combinations possible. Finally, he hit upon a pale yellow background with grey letters.

There it was—the date in the seal said 08-07-01. Dax's eyes stopped for a split second, then he blinked several times and rubbed his eyes. He knew what he saw, but was not ready to confirm it. He stood up, stretched, and walked over to Brand, who was reading the paper. "Anything yet?"

"Not yet. Mind if I have some of that?"

"Well, I'd rather you get to finishing whatever you are doing so we can go home."

"I will, but I need a minute to rest my eyes." Brand handed over the paper. Dax knew he had to be really careful now. He pretended to read parts of the paper, but he was only pretending. When he got to the obit section, he memorized two names, ages, and where they were from before moving on to the next sections.

When he went back to the computer, Brand was still on the phone. "We can't be sure Boss, but we think he found something in the notary seal on the certificate. Maybe you'd better sit with him now."

"Okay, thanks."

Brand decided to wait just a few more minutes before moving in on Dax.

Dax was thinking about the date on the seal of Tom Dittmer's birth certificate. He was trying to reason out why the day the guy died was the date on the certificate. Mistake by the notary? Had someone changed the date? Was it a fake certificate?

It took Dax a few more minutes to find the other two groupings of the names he had memorized and to find all the hospital birth records for them. He had just put them each in a file like he had done with the Tom Dittmer one. Brand came over and sat next to him.

"Well, what are you finding?"

"I'm really not sure what I am finding or if what I am finding is fake."

"Well, why don't you tell me and we can decide together."

"Okay, here goes." Dax showed Brand the Tom Dittmer seal on the computer with the date of 08-07-01.

Brand said, "How could that be? The guy was born in 1949 not 2001."

"That's what I mean. Maybe the birth certificate is a fake?"

"What do you think?" Brand thought for a minute. He didn't want to say anything until he made a call.

"I'll be right back." Brand called for the Marine and asked if he could talk to the Secretary of Defense.

"I'll get him on the phone for you. Be back in just a minute."

Dax began checking the other two names from today's Washington paper. Margaret Lewis, age 64, retired, and Andrew Morgan, age 23, school teacher. Margaret would have been born in 1937 and Andrew in 1978. Margaret took a while to find. It seems a lot of parents liked the name Margie back then. He left the background the same as when he found Tom Dittmer's certificate. It worked. Margie's date in the seal said 08-10-04. Now Dax was feeling uneasy. This meant the first one was not a mistake, but did not rule out the possibility of it being fake. He had to follow through. Andrew Morgan—notary seal—definitely said D.O.D. 08-10-01.

Dax quickly shut his eyes. He had found the link but wasn't sure what it meant. He knew it would only be a minute before Brand came back. He stepped over to a couple of the other computers and printed off some other certificates. He stashed them inside his shirt just as Brand came over.

"Well, we have an audience with the Secretary of Defense in five minutes. You need to tell him what you have found and leave nothing out."

"Okay by me." The three of them sat in a room just outside the President's oval office.

"Nice to meet you, sir, Dax said."

"Please sit down, Dax, and you too, Brand." It was obvious to Dax that this was not the first time Brand had met the Secretary of Defense.

# CHAPTER 17

They talked for over two hours. Dax explained what he saw in the notary seals on the birth certificates. They definitely said D.O.D. followed by the date the person died. He stated the three names he found and how he just picked them at random. The Secretary listened quietly.

"What sort of theory do you have about what you saw?" he asked.

"Well, none, really. I think they are probably fake birth certificates or someone altered them for some unknown reason." Dax then said, "Can I ask you a couple of questions, sir."

"Sure, but I can't promise I have an answer."

"Okay. My first question is, What does the Department of Defense have to do with birth certificates? Second, Why would the date of death be on a birth certificate if it is a real one? And third, If the birth certificates are real, how did someone know the day these people were born, what date they were going to die—especially when they die in a car accident? No one can predict that!"

"I see. Those are valid questions and ones that I would ask myself, but for right now, I do not have those answers for you."

Brand and Dax shook hands with the Secretary and said their good-byes. They were drivin' to the airport immediately and flown back to Denver.

On the plane, Dax was wide awake and started firing questions at Brand. "What do you think? Did we find what they were looking for? I'm thinking we did. Otherwise, we would still be there."

"Don't keep thinking about it. Apparently we did find it, or like you said, we would still be there. I doubt they will tell us anymore."

"But, Brand, for God's sake, if people can find out when they are going to die...."

# CHAPTER 18

It had been two weeks since Dax and Brand had returned from D.C. Dax had not even talked to Brand since then. Dax's life was back on track. He went to work on construction jobs around the Denver area. He spent his nights at the bar and weekends at the golf course and then the bar.

"Hi, Dad. What are you doing?"

"Hi, Dade. What are you doing?"

"Well, for one thing, I'm calling you not to ask for money—how about that?"

Dax laughed. "And the second thing?"

"Well, do you remember when I called you and asked you for some stuff on DNA?"

"Yes, I remember."

"Well, I got an A on the paper! And I got to meet some real important people because of what I wrote. How about that?"

"Yeah, how about that? That's great! Who exactly did you meet?"

"He was a real big army guy by the name of Powell. I can't remember his first name, but he was really nice and asked me lots of questions about my paper, and Mom took a picture of me and him together. It was in the newspaper here."

"Okay, okay. Sounds like it was a pretty big deal. Do I get to see your famous picture in the paper?"

"Yep, Mom put them in the mail to you today."

Dax was quiet for a few seconds to see if Dade had any more to say.

"Dade, did you tell Mr. Powell where you got the information for your paper?"

"You mean General Powell?"

"Yes, General Powell."

"Well, sure! I told him you sent me a bunch of stuff."

"Did he ask you where I got the stuff?"

"Yep! I told him you were really smart and you knew a lot of this stuff already. Dad, I gotta go now—but maybe you would want to send me some money for getting that A?"

Dax chuckled. "Sure, Dade. You earned it—but don't tell your sister—okay, bud?"

"Okay, Dad. Love you. Bye!"

Dax hung up the phone and got ready for the golf tournament JR was sponsoring today. About five minutes later, the doorbell rang. Dax went to the door, thinking it was JR to pick him up. He was very surprised to see none other than General Powell standing there. Powell was out of uniform and quickly introduced himself and extended his hand.

"Good morning, sir," Dax said as he shook the General's hand. The General smiled.

"May I come in?"

"Sure."

They sat down in the upstairs living room, which the landlord always kept neat as a pin. General Powell was even bigger in life than he appeared on the TV news. He filled the chair and had a commanding presence.

"Dax, do you know why I am here?

"Not exactly, sir, but I think I can guess. This has something to do with the paper my son wrote?"

"Well, yes and no. I am here to ask you what you think you found while you were at the Pentagon?"

"How did you know that I was at....Oh, never mind. I don't really know what I found, not really."

"You know what you think you found though, don't you?"

Dax didn't know what he should say. He just sat and looked at the General and waited. He was sure the General had more to say.

"Here's the thing, Dax. The information you sent your son was top secret, classified, military scientific data about DNA the country and all countries must not know about. Every piece of DNA analysis done by the government since 1900 was in the material you sent him."

"But I thought we only learned about DNA in the 70's or 80's?"

"That is exactly what we intended. The government allows information to be shared with the general public when we think they can handle it."

Dax's mind was racing. "Are you saying that the government let people be convicted of crimes they didn't commit before it came out to the public? That the government knew it was possible to use DNA to prove someone's innocence or guilt as early as 1900?"

"Dax, sometimes decisions have to be made that protect more people than the few that are hurt by them." Both men were silent for a minute.

"Dax, I need to know that you can keep what you found at the Pentagon to yourself. You must never mention anything you saw or think you figured out on your own. I need you to promise me you will never say a word to anyone, ever."

Dax was in shock. What the General had just told him confirmed that what he saw on the birth certificates was real. Every person's Date-of-Death was known the day they were born.

The doorbell rang. Dax stood up, but before he headed to the door, he turned to the General and said, "You have my word."

The General stood, shook Dax's hand and said, "I will show myself out the back door. Thank you. Oh, good luck at the golf tournament today."

"Thanks, but how did you know I am...."

The doorbell rang again. The General went out the back door and Dax opened the front door for JR.

"You ready? We're late for shots at the first tee!"

# CHAPTER 19

It was Friday, September 11, 2001. The bar opened at 7:00 AM. Judy was working. Sherry was in the back doing the books. So far, only Dax, Dick, and Jerry were at the bar. They were watching some morning news show when suddenly the show was interrupted.

Tom Brokaw came on the screen.

"Ladies and gentlemen of the United States, we have just learned that a United Airlines plane has crashed into one of the twin towers in New York City. We will now go live to coverage in New York...."

Judy changed all of the TVs in the bar to the same channel. The five people sat glued to the television. They watched in horror as did the rest of the world when the second plane hit the second tower, and then as the third plane being diverted from the White House crashed, and the fourth plane struck the Pentagon.

Dax shivered and had a sick feeling inside. He sat there quietly drinking—drink after drink after drink...until it was dark outside. For the world, time stood still that day, but time does not stop, and so life went on.

Christmas came, and Dax was helping JR set up Christmas dinner at the bar for the folks who don't have family to be with. Very unexpectedly, Brand walked into the bar.

"What are you doing here on Christmas day?"

"Hi, Dax. I came to give you this." Brand took Dax's hand and put something cold made of metal in it and he closed Dax's hand around it.

"I gotta go. Don't lose this. Somebody may come for it someday."

Dax didn't open his hand right away. He just told Brand good-bye and put the object in his pants pocket. Later that night, when Dax got home, he pulled the mail from the mailbox. There was a package from Chicago. He figured it was Dade's school paper.

Dax undressed down to his shorts and laid down on the floor. He tried not to think about everything that had happened since Brand had first called everyone into his office and showed them the large jewelry box with the crosses.

He got up and took the object Brand had given him out of his pants pocket. It was the last cross they had found. It had a note attached to it.

All computers at the Pentagon were destroyed when the plane hit the building. The other crosses were recovered. The twelve of you who have them must keep them safe. They are not to be destroyed. Someone will come for them someday.

Dax took the cross and the note and went to put them with his high school yearbook. He opened the book to where he had put the two birth certificates he smuggled out of the Pentagon, but they were gone. In their place was a note with Brand's handwriting.

Sorry, Dax. This is for your own good. Brand

Dax put the cross in the drawer and closed it. He wondered how many years he would have to guard it.